M000028175

AMERICANOS AND ASSAULT

CUP OF JO BOOK 7

KELLY HASHWAY

To Ayla with love

CHAPTER ONE

Cup of Jo is busier than usual Friday morning. I don't think I've sat down or even slowed down once since opening. When I set out to have my own coffee shop, lovingly named Cup of Jo since my name is Joanna Coffee, I dreamed I'd be this successful. And now here I am, co-owner with my amazing baker of a boyfriend, Camden Turner. I've known Cam for my entire life, and we've been dating for months. He's made the move back to Bennett Falls, Pennsylvania better in so many ways. Let's just say I fled to California for a while to recover after my ex, Detective Quentin Perry, cheated on me with my ex best friend, Samantha Shaw, who happens to be Samantha Perry now. Did I mention she owns Bouquets of Love, the flower shop right next door to Cup of Jo?

But somehow, I manage to stay sane. Mostly because Cam is amazing, my younger sister, Mo, always has my back, and the residents in town all sided with me in the breakup. It also doesn't hurt that Quentin has needed my help on numerous occasions solving cases he can't crack. He went from hating that I made him look bad to asking for my help to avoid looking like I one-upped him.

I finish ringing up an order when Mickey Baldwin, town gossip and my best customer, steps up to the counter. "What can I get for you, Mickey?" He spends hours here each day after working the night shift as a custodian at the local high school.

"Another Americano, please," he says, motioning to the special's board. I have a chalkboard theme going on in Cup of Jo, based on that exact board. Everything is black and white but with pops of neon chalk colors. "I can't believe I've never had an Americano until you put it on special today."

It's really a simple drink for people who don't like straight espresso since the only two ingredients are espresso and water. Personally, I prefer the strength of espresso, but it's watered down counterpart, the Americano, is a big hit with a lot of people in town if the number of drinks I've served so far today is any indication. "You've got it, Mickey."

I start making his drink when out of the corner of my eye I see him lean over the counter and wave me back to him. Cup in hand, I step toward him. He makes a show of looking around to ensure no one is trying to listen in. Then he cups his mouth with his hand and whispers, "I saw police cars heading to Fantasy Fitness about two hours ago."

I'm not sure why he's whispering if this happened hours ago. Mickey is the main source of information in this town, and he usually uses my coffee shop as his center stage. I place his cup on the counter. "How many people have you told this to?" I ask.

He points a finger at me. "Nothing to actually tell yet. I was hoping a certain police detective called you with the scoop."

I shake my head. "Sorry, Mickey. I haven't heard from Detective Perry today." Which is why I'm having a good day so far. Quentin has apologized for his actions, and we get along okay now, but I'm not going to call him a friend anytime soon.

Mickey's face falls. "Okay, then I guess I'll just take the Americano and another muffin."

I know what he's doing. He's prolonging his time here in hopes that Quentin will show up, and he can get some dirt on what happened at the gym. "I don't want to get a call from your physician about all the baked goods and caffeine you consume here." I turn around to get his Americano.

"I know, but can you really blame me? Cam's baking is too good, and I've loved every drink you've ever made me."

I place his drink on the counter. "How about a bran muffin? At least that's a little healthier than double chocolate chip."

Mickey's shoulders slump. "Only if I can get a chocolate stick for my coffee."

"That kind of defeats the purpose, Mickey." I ring him up, grabbing a chocolate stick from the jar next to the register and placing it in his Americano. "Want Cam to warm the muffin?"

"Yes, please." Mickey places a single in the tip mug and smiles before taking his coffee back to his table.

"I'll get the muffin," Robin, one of my only two employees, says, joining me behind the counter.

"Thanks, Robin."

"No problem. I had to get away from Jamar. If he spun me one more time, I was going to lose my breakfast." She rolls her eyes.

Jamar is my other employee as well as my neighbor and friend. He has a tendency to perform for the customers by dancing with them. I guess he brought Robin into his act today.

The door to Cup of Jo opens, drawing my attention. Samantha walks in looking very unhappy. She's a few months pregnant now, and she and Quentin recently started seeing a therapist since Samantha announced she hates being pregnant. She's not the type to sacrifice of herself or think of anyone but herself. Thankfully, her mother will be watching the baby after it's born, and Samantha will be going back to work.

She walks up to the register. "Oh, Jo, have you heard from Quentin?"

"No, I haven't." Why does everyone assume I know where that man is? I purposely try to avoid him.

She blows out a puff of air, making a few strands of

blonde hair fly up from her forehead. "He was called out of bed at four in the morning when the custodial crew opened up the gym and found the dead body." She says it like it was a total inconvenience to her to have the phone wake her at that hour. Never mind someone died.

I lower my voice, modeling proper volume when discussing cases that shouldn't be talked about in public. "Samantha, I don't think Quentin would want you talking about that in here."

"Well, then he should call me. I mean look at me." She holds her arms out at her sides. "I'm as big as a house."

Truth be told, she's not that big at all. "No, you're not. You look great. In fact, you're glowing." I'm laying it on thick, but I want her to stop with the theatrics and go back to her own store.

"You think so?" she asks me. "I feel like a whale."

"It's all in your head. Did you want to order something?"

"Maybe a piece of pie. Or a donut." She bites her lower lip. "Crumb cake?" She huffs. "I can't even think straight. I'm so tired."

And hungry, apparently. "I'll see what Cam has fresh out of the oven." I hurry into the kitchen, mostly to get away from her.

"Hey, beautiful," Cam says when I enter. He's pulling a coffee cake out of the oven.

It's amazing how he can make me blush when he's

5

also witnessed my awkward preteen years. "Samantha's here."

"Oh." He places the cake on a cooling rake and walks over to me. "Let Robin or Jamar handle her."

"Too late. She told me there was a dead body discovered at the gym this morning. And Mickey told me he saw police cars at Fantasy Fitness, so putting the two together, I'd say someone was found dead there this morning."

Cam smirks. "Not your best sleuthing since that was pretty obvious."

I bob one shoulder. "I can't always be on my A game."

He leans forward and kisses me on the lips. "What can I do for you?"

"Samantha wants something to eat but doesn't know what."

"I'll handle it. Feel free to hide out here until she leaves." He turns and slices a large piece of the coffee cake, which he puts in a to-go container.

"No, I can't hide from her and Quentin all my life, no matter how much I'd like to." Somehow, I wound up catering their wedding. I can't get rid of them because they always manage to pull me into their drama. Quentin nearly broke down to me just a few weeks ago. Neither one of them has any boundaries, at least not where I'm concerned.

"How did I know I'd find you in here?" Mo asks, walking into the kitchen.

I turn to face her. "Well, I'm assuming you saw Samantha out there and knew I'd be as far away as I could get."

"She has the roundest belly. Have you noticed?" Mo gestures with her hands. "It's like a mini basketball in there." She drops her arms to the side and stares at me in horror. "Can you imagine what it will be like when pregnancy brain kicks in? That woman is dumb as dirt to begin with."

"Stop it." I swat at her arm. "She's not stupid; she's just incredibly naïve." Growing up, I stood up for Samantha when other kids picked on her for her naivety. That was before she stabbed me in the back.

"I'll be right back," Cam says, carrying the coffee cake out of the kitchen.

"So," Mo says, "you and Cam have been having a lot of solo dinners this week. What's up?"

She's not wrong. My apartment is usually the place to be at dinnertime. Jamar typically comes over as well as Mo and sometimes her boyfriend, Wes. I just haven't felt up to crowds lately. Not since I had the realization that I want Cam to propose to me. I guess I thought dining alone would give him the opportunity to do so. But maybe he's not thinking about marriage.

I shrug. "I just wanted a quiet week, I suppose."

She narrows her eyes at me. "Spill. I can tell there's something on your mind."

If I tell her the truth, she'll scream so loud everyone in Cup of Jo will think someone's been murdered back here. But I also can't lie to my sister. She'd see right through it.

I grab her arm and pull her to the back door. "Not a word."

She mimes zipping her lips.

I check to make sure no one is coming into the kitchen before whispering, "I was kind of hoping Cam was going to pop the question."

Mo slaps her hand over her mouth and lets out a muffled squeal.

"Don't get too excited. He hasn't asked me, and I don't think he's planning to anytime soon."

Mo lowers her hand. "Then you should ask him. Women can do that, you know. And everyone in town is just waiting for the day it happens because we all know it will."

"I don't think I want to be the one to ask."

Mo crosses her arms and cocks her head. "Why not?"

"Because Cam has never said no to me. What if I ask and he's not ready, but he says yes because he doesn't want to disappoint me. I want him to ask so I know it's what he wants."

She takes both my hands in hers. "If you can't tell how much that man loves you by the look of pure bliss in his eyes when he sees you, you're blind, Jo. I know for certain it would make his entire world if you asked him."

"Asked who?" Cam says, walking into the kitchen. "Samantha's gone by the way." He jerks a thumb over his shoulder.

"Oh, good," I say, letting go of Mo's hands so Cam doesn't think something is up.

My efforts are futile because he eyes us suspiciously. "What's going on in here? You two look like you're plotting something."

I think quickly. "No, I have to remember to call my dad later so I can ask him about this new brand of espresso beans he's been using." He told me about them a few days ago and did promise to let me know how his customers liked them, so this isn't exactly a lie. I never said that's what Mo and I were discussing. I only said I have to remember to follow up with my dad about the beans.

"Oh."

"Jo?" Jamar pokes his head into the kitchen.

"Yeah?" I say, thankful for the distraction. I don't like keeping things from Cam.

Jamar scrunches his face. "You're not going to be happy to hear this, but Quentin is here to see you."

He's right. I'm not happy in the least. Especially if he didn't go see his wife before coming to Cup of Jo. She'll be in here making a scene in no time if that's the case.

"He asked to speak to you in private," Jamar adds. "What do you want me to tell him?"

"Nothing. I'll handle it. Thanks, Jamar."

He nods and heads out.

"Want me to come with you?" Cam asks.

"No, it's okay. We both know what this is about. I'll fill you in as soon as he leaves." I turn to Mo, realizing I don't know what brought her here. "Did you need something?"

"Nope. I came here because I'm bored. Wes called out today. He wasn't feeling well after the seafood we had last night. I think he ate some bad shrimp."

"Aw, and you're lost without him?" I tease.

She gives me a challenging look, and I know better than to push her with the dirt she has on me right now.

"Cam, can you get Mo some of that coffee cake, please?" I say before disappearing through the kitchen door.

Quentin is standing by the counter. The fact that he didn't take a seat at the corner table like he usually does when he needs to talk tells me this isn't something he wants to risk others overhearing.

I motion for him to follow me back into the office. "What's going on?" I ask, closing the door behind him.

"Well, Mickey asked me about the death at the gym, so I'm assuming you know about it," he says.

"Actually, you can thank your wife for that one. She was in here a little bit ago."

Quentin runs a hand through his hair. "I guess I should have expected that. I took off in such a hurry this morning I forgot to remind her not to say anything about the case."

It's ridiculous that he has to tell her that every single time he gets a case. She should be aware by now. "What's with all the secrecy if Mickey's talking about it out there?" I ask.

Quentin leans against the filing cabinet. "We have a new chief of police at the station."

"I heard. What's he like?"

"His name is Owen Harvey. He transferred here from central Jersey. He's strict and definitely trying to prove his worth." He crosses his arms. "And he is emphatically against using consultants."

I laugh. "Are you calling me a consultant? Because despite promises, I have yet to be paid for my services to the Bennett Falls PD."

"I know. I was going to put it through for the last case since I was interim chief at the time, but things were a little crazy, and when I remembered, I wasn't interim chief anymore."

By crazy he means Samantha was crying about how she doesn't want to be a mother. I won't deny it was intense. Quentin has his hands full with her. I wave a hand in the air. "Doesn't matter." I don't get involved with these cases for money. I do it because dating Quentin for years gave me this insatiable need to solve murders. It's become almost an obsession. "If the new chief doesn't want consultants, why are you here?"

Quentin shoves his hands in his pockets. "I can't seem to focus lately. With so much going on in my home life, my brain is scattered."

"You need my help."

He nods. "But you can't let anyone know you're helping me solve this murder."

So it was definitely a murder. "This was a lot easier

when I went behind your back and solved your cases for you."

"I wouldn't object if you did that this time around."

I narrow my eyes at him. "You don't even want credit?"

"I'm just trying to survive day to day." He stands up straight. "Will you help me?"

We both know what I'm going to say, but it's still fun to watch him squirm, so I pretend to weigh my options before finally giving in and saying, "Let's solve a murder."

CHAPTER TWO

Quentin couldn't look more relieved. "Okay, but remember this has to stay between us. You can't say anything to anyone else."

I cock my head at him because he's well aware I'm going to tell Cam. I'm not about to keep a secret like this from him. What would Cam think if I was sneaking around with my ex? What would the town think if I was sneaking around with Quentin when he's married with a child on the way? "I have to tell Cam. That's not even an option. And I'll need Mo at some point. I can't do the kind of online digging that she can." She's a wiz on the computer, and I'd be lost without her. Of course, she'll tell Wes because they're always together. And then there's Jamar, who typically comes for dinner a few times a week and is present when I discuss cases with Cam and Mo. This is going to spiral out of control in no time.

Quentin drags a hand through his hair again and groans.

"You're going to make yourself prematurely bald if you keep that up," I say.

He lowers his arm. "I'm not going to go bald. Jo, I need you to focus right now. My job could be on the line. I'm already in hot water for not accepting the position as chief of police."

Quentin couldn't stand being behind a desk when there were murderers on the loose. To be honest, I think he gained the most respect from me when he turned down that promotion and chose to go back to being a detective because he felt he could do the most good in that position.

"I'm not going to do anything to get you in trouble, but I have to tell my core group. They aren't going to say a word to anyone else. You don't have to worry about that."

"Core group? Cam and Mo, you mean?"

"And possibly Wes and Jamar, but that's it." I wave my hands in front of me.

Quentin throws his head back and stares at the ceiling of my office. I swear he can't bear to look at me right now without completely losing it. I have to admit I get great satisfaction from knowing I can annoy him this much. I may have moved past his cheating, but I'll never forget it, nor will I allow him to forget it.

He waits several seconds before returning his gaze to

me. "Jo, I don't think you understand what's at stake here."

"No, I don't think *you* do." I stab my index finger into his chest. "I'm not going to let anyone in this town think I'm running around with you behind Cam's back."

"You are not telling the entire town about this!" He throws his hands in the air.

"No, I'm not. I'm not an idiot, Quentin. I'll let everyone believe I'm conducting my own investigation behind your back. We both know I've done that enough for it to be believable."

He scoffs in agreement. "That could work. I'll stop by your place if I have any information for you. That way no one other than Jamar will see me."

"Or you could call or text me like a normal person." I hate how he just shows up at my apartment unannounced. The last thing I want to see when I get home from a long day's work is his sorry figure slumped over on my welcome mat.

"I could do that. But swear it's just Mo and Jamar you'll include in this."

"And Cam."

"Naturally," he says with annoyance.

"And possibly Wes. Don't forget him. He's been quite helpful too since he has the same skill set as Mo."

"If they have the same skill set, why do you need both of them?" he asks, sounding exasperated.

"Because I'm not going to tell my little sister to put her relationship on hold so you can solve a case. Sorry, but that's not happening." Mo hates Quentin enough as it is. He really doesn't need to give her any more reason to dislike him or to lash out at him in public. She won't hesitate to humiliate him in front of the entire town.

"I hate this," Quentin says, crossing his arms.

"Are you going to keep whining, or are you going to give me the details I need to start investigating?" I put my hands on my hips, done with our back-and-forth verbal sparring match.

"Fine." He takes his notebook out of his pocket and flips it open. "The victim's name is Sabrina Kincade. She's thirty-four years old and a fitness instructor at Fantasy Fitness."

I take out my phone and jot Sabrina's name in my Notes app. "Go on."

"That's really all I can tell you."

I lower my phone and glare at him. "You haven't told me anything. Her name is nothing to go on, Quentin. I could have gotten this much information from Mickey." I throw my hand out in the direction of the door. "Should I go ask him about Sabrina and how and when she was killed?"

"All right. Calm down." He shakes his head.

"Oh, I'm sorry. Is this too much work for you, Detective? Because you can feel free to solve the case on your own. It's no sweat off my back."

He huffs. "Sabrina taught self-defense classes at the gym, but ironically enough, she was assaulted."

"What was the cause of death?" I ask.

"I don't have the coroner's report yet, but judging by the state of her skull, I'm going to say blunt force trauma to the head."

"From like a free weight or something?" I ask.

He shrugs. "Most likely. The forensics team is still at the crime scene collecting evidence and taking photos."

"And you'll have copies of those photos for me later, right?"

"You're not going to make this easy on me, are you?" he asks.

"I would, but you don't pay me enough—or you know, at all."

He clears his throat instead of responding.

"Time of death is still unknown?"

"Again, I have to wait for the coroner's report for a more definitive time, but we're assuming sometime between nine last night and four o'clock this morning."

That means the body was discovered at four o'clock this morning. "Samantha said an employee discovered the body."

He nods, but his jaw is clenched.

"You really need to make it clear to her that she can't talk about these cases." She's always coming into Cup of Jo and blurting out things the BFPD does not want the public to know.

"I've tried. She hasn't been easy to deal with since she became pregnant. Her hormones are out of control, and when I try to tell her not to do something, she starts crying and saying I don't love her as much as I love the baby."

"I see marriage counseling is going well." I don't mean to sound as snarky as I do. "Sorry."

He waves a hand in the air. "I guess I should have expected this. It's not like I didn't know she could be…"

I'm really interested to see how he's going to finish that sentence. I have a few choice words, but I don't see Quentin using any of them to describe the love of his life.

He sighs. "She doesn't always understand things the way other people do. It's something I've always found endearing, but now it's become a little tiresome."

"Does she still have you running out to the food store in the middle of the night to satisfy her cravings?"

"Luckily, no. I had her make a list of every food that sounded even remotely good, and I fully stocked the house. Whenever she eats something, I buy more. So far, it's been working."

"Glad to hear it. Back to the case."

"I really don't have anything else to tell you. There isn't much to go on yet."

"And I'm assuming I won't get near the gym anytime soon either."

He shakes his head. "It's an active crime scene at the moment. We should be able to get everything we need soon so the gym can reopen, but the women's locker room will most likely remain off-limits until the case is closed."

I furrow my brow. "Women's locker room?"

"Yeah, that's where the body was discovered. The custodial crew was cleaning the place before they opened for the day."

"Do you know the name of the person who found the body?" He or she would be a great person to start with to get answers.

"Yeah." Quentin flips a page in his little notebook. "Logan Ross."

I jot his name down in my Notes app as well. "Great. I'll start with him."

"But you can't—"

I hold up a hand to stop him. "I can't tell anyone I'm helping you with the case. I got it. This isn't my first investigation, Quentin. Give me a little credit."

"If I didn't, I wouldn't have come to you for help." He turns and walks out of the office.

"Always a pleasure," I call after him.

To my surprise, Mo is leaning against the counter, a coffee in hand. "Well, that took a while. I'm on my second cup." She raises her mug.

I quickly text her both Sabrina Kincade's and Logan Ross's names. When her phone buzzes in her pocket, I say, "I need addresses for both, and anything you can find out about the woman."

Mo nods. "Any reason for the secrecy?" she whispers.

"I'll explain at dinner tonight. I'm making pasta fagioli."

"Tell me there will be garlic bread to go with it, and I'll be there with the wine."

"There will be garlic bread, and if Wes is feeling better, you can bring him."

She smiles. "Great. Now, I should get back to work if I still want to have a job to go to each day." She turns on her heel and walks out, placing a tip in the tip mug on the way since she never actually pays.

"Everything okay?" Jamar asks me as he preps an espresso.

"You busy tonight?"

Cam walks out of the kitchen at that exact moment. "Jo, asking out an employee at work when I'm only feet away?" He smiles and wraps an arm around me.

Jamar's face goes pale. "I—"

"You're coming over for dinner," I say. "Mo and possibly Wes will be there as well. We have dinner and drinks taken care of."

"Then I guess that leaves dessert up to me," Jamar says.

"That's what I was hoping you'd say."

Around three in the afternoon, my phone vibrates with a text from Mo. I read the screen to see she has addresses for both Sabrina Kincade and Logan Ross. I quickly thank her before removing my apron.

"Jamar, Cam and I are going to need to head out for a bit."

Jamar's gaze goes to the coffee cup clock on the wall. "Do you want Robin and I to close up Cup of Jo if you're not back?"

"Would you mind?" I ask. "We'll pay you extra for it."

Jamar squeezes my arm. "You're already the best bosses either of us has ever had. If you go doing things like paying us extra for simply cleaning coffee machines, you may never get rid of us."

"That's the plan," I say with a smile.

"Is dinner still on?" he asks.

"Yes, definitely. I have something to discuss with all of you." I contemplate winking, but that would be really suspicious and possibly creepy since I'm not the winking type.

Jamar bobs his head in understanding. "Got it." I should have known he'd pick up on the reason for dinner without much explanation. It's not like any of this is new to us at this point.

After smiling at him, I go into the kitchen to collect Cam, and we head for Logan Ross's house.

I figured after finding a dead body, he'd be tied up at the police station for a while. But it's been almost twelve hours since Quentin was called to the crime scene, and since Mr. Ross's workday is likely long over by now, there's a good chance he's home trying to pretend this day never happened.

I pull up to a small raised ranch on a side street off of Sandalwood Road. Sandalwood is the only street in Bennett Falls with a one-lane bridge. I once got stuck before the bridge and had to wait for a funeral precession. Needless to say, I avoid this road whenever possible because of that experience. Maybe it's all the coffee I drink, but I don't like sitting idle, literally or figuratively speaking.

We get out of my Honda Accord and walk up the steps to the front door. Cam rings the doorbell, giving me an expression that says, "Here goes nothing."

When no one answers, Cam says, "Do you think there's any way he's still tied up at the station?"

I'm tempted to text Quentin, but I can't see how Mr. Ross would still be there hours later. He could've given his statement countless times by now. Unless the police have a reason to suspect him of something, but at this early stage in the investigation, I don't see how they'd have enough evidence to pin this on anyone.

"He has to be here. Maybe he's sleeping." Exhaustion could have taken over once he got home after the ordeal.

I take out my phone and check Mo's text. There's no phone number for either name I sent her. I dial her and put the call on speaker.

"This is Maura Coffee. How can I assist you?" she answers.

"Hmm, I thought I was calling my little sister," I say.

She laughs. "Sorry. I've been busy, and I answered as if it were the work line. What's up, Jo?"

"Did you happen to find a phone number for Logan Ross? Cam and I are at his place now, but there's no answer."

"Hang on."

I hear her fingers flying across the keys of her laptop. I do my best not to tap my foot while I wait.

"Okay, I'll text the number to you. Is that all? I'm really swamped today with Wes being out, and I don't want to be late for dinner."

"Yeah, go. Thanks, Mo." I wait for the text to come, and then I click on the number to call it.

A grumbled curse comes from inside the house, and then a groggy voice answers, "Hello?"

Looks like the phone woke him when the doorbell didn't.

"Mr. Ross?" I ask.

"Yeah."

"Hi, I'm sorry to bother you, but I was hoping we could talk for a few minutes about Sabrina Kincade."

"Who is this? I already told the police everything."

I've pretended to be a news reporter before, but I don't want to overplay that card, so I level with him. "My name is Joanna Coffee. I own Cup of Jo on Main Street."

"Haven't been there. There's a coffee truck right outside the gym."

Not a bad plan on the coffee truck owner's part. Get people revved up to work out each morning. He probably makes a good amount of money doing it. "Right, well,

23

I'm somewhat of an amateur sleuth. I'm hoping I can help solve the mystery behind Sabrina Kincade's death."

"I already gave my statement to the cops."

"I know, but I work better on my own. The police aren't always happy to have help, if you know what I mean."

He laughs but says, "Look, I'm tired. It's been a long day. Maybe another time." He hangs up.

"Now what?" Cam asks me.

I sit down on the front steps, determined not to leave without speaking to Logan Ross. "We wait for him to come out and talk to us."

CHAPTER THREE

I'm actually worried about missing dinner. We've been on the front porch for two hours. Jamar and Robin are most likely cleaning up Cup of Jo right now. I text Jamar and Mo to tell them dinner will be a little later than I thought. Mo has a key to my place, so I tell her to go ahead and make herself at home until we get there. Luckily, pasta fagioli doesn't take long to make.

A car pulls into the driveway, and a pizza delivery guy gets out with a box in hand. I smile at Cam as I stand up. I hand the guy a twenty-dollar bill. "Keep the change," I say, earning myself a big smile and an excited, "Thank you!"

"Sneaky, Jo Coffee. Very sneaky," Cam says with a laugh.

The delivery guy is still in the driveway when I ring the bell, which is what I want because it will mean Logan Ross will actually open the door this time. The front door opens just as the car pulls out of the driveway. The man who answered looks at me in confusion.

"Logan Ross?" I ask. "I'm Joanna Coffee. I paid for your pizza, so how about you talk to my boyfriend and me for a few minutes?"

Logan is in his thirties with blond hair and greener than green eyes. "You paid for my pizza so I would talk to you?"

"Yes, and we only want to know how you found Sabrina Kincade this morning. That's it. I swear."

Logan takes the pizza box from me. "Come on inside."

"Thank you," I say as he steps aside to let Cam and me pass.

"I'm Camden Turner. I run Cup of Jo with Jo here." Cam shakes Logan's free hand.

"You guys want a slice?" Logan asks, bringing us to the kitchen.

"No, thank you. We have dinner plans. I promise we don't intend to take up much of your time." We've already been here for hours, waiting on his front steps.

Logan places the pizza box on the stove and grabs a slice, which he puts on a paper towel. He brings it to the kitchen table and sits, gesturing for us to take seats as well. "I got to work at a quarter to four this morning, like always. The gym opens at six, so I have to have my cleaning done before that. My rounds take about two hours. I'm usually finishing up when the first customers are coming in."

"Is Sabrina usually there early?" I ask.

Logan shakes his head. "She works afternoons and evenings. I've actually never met her. Her picture is on the wall, though. All the trainers have their pictures and bios on the wall for customers to peruse. Most have won weightlifting competitions or other things of that nature. My boss says it's great for business for people to see those accomplishments displayed like that."

If Sabrina wasn't supposed to be there in the morning, it means she was killed before she left work on Thursday evening. And it would have been after everyone else left for the day. "Where was she when you found her?" I ask, even though Quentin told me it was in the women's locker room.

"I went into the locker rooms to clean the showers. Sabrina was on the floor in the shower area of the women's locker room."

"So her attacker snuck up on her while she was showering," Cam says.

Logan bites his pizza and shakes his head. "She was still fully clothed."

Hmm, it would have made sense that someone jumped her when she was in a compromising position, like naked in a shower, maybe even with shampoo in her eyes. "I heard Sabrina was a self-defense instructor," I say. "How do you think someone got the upper hand on her?"

"My guess is they snuck up on her from behind," Logan says before taking another bite of his dinner. "She looked really fit. Her biceps might have been bigger than mine." He holds up his arm. He's not huge by any means, but he's not scrawny either. If Sabrina's arms were more muscular than his, than she was in incredible shape.

"I guess that would make sense. Was she in a shower stall?"

"No," Logan says with his mouth full. "She was in the shower area, but not in a stall. I thought maybe she was on her way to shower when she was attacked."

"Were any of the showers running?" Cam asks.

Logan's brow furrows. "No. I don't know if she had any things in a stall, either. Like a towel and change of clothes. I didn't look. When I found her body and saw all the blood, I called the cops. I was afraid to touch anything or even move until they got there."

I can't blame him. I have no doubt Quentin grilled him with questions and made him feel like a criminal. He doesn't have the best people skills. "Did you notice anything else that stood out to you?"

"Like what?" Logan asks before breaking off a piece of crust and popping it into his mouth.

"I don't know. Open lockers or belongings on the benches." I haven't ever stepped foot inside Fantasy Fitness, so I don't know what the locker rooms even look like.

"There was a cell phone on the ledge of the sink."

Probably Sabrina's. That's good. That means

Quentin has it and will know if anyone was meeting Sabrina at the gym.

"Are there cameras in the gym anywhere?" Cam asks.

"Yeah," Logan says, "but not in the locker rooms, of course."

Of course. "Still, that might tell us if anyone else was in the gym at the time Sabrina was murdered."

Logan shrugs and wipes his hands on his napkin. "That's really all I know. I think the detective who questioned me thought I was withholding information since I had so little to tell him, but there was no one else there and nothing seemed out of place."

"Do you know if all the free weights were accounted for?" I ask.

Logan nods. "I cleaned them all myself. I always clean the gym equipment first. I have to disinfect all surfaces."

I bite my lip to keep from groaning, but it's entirely possible that Logan cleaned evidence off the murder weapon without knowing it. The only good news is if someone did take a free weight and bring it to the locker room, the cameras should have caught it. "Mr. Ross, thank you for your time. We'll let you finish your dinner in peace." I stand up, and Cam follows my lead.

"Thanks for the pizza," Logan says, walking us back to the front door.

"You're welcome." He's had a rough day, and I'm not sure the Bennett Falls PD thought to give the man any food.

"So, what do you think?" Cam asks as I drive to my apartment.

"I think this murder was definitely premeditated. Someone waited for an opportunity to get Sabrina alone, and they knew to sneak up on her."

"Then not a random attack at all. Think Quentin will share the contents of Sabrina's phone with us?"

"If he wants this case solved he will."

I nearly fall over when we walk into my apartment to find the table set and Mo and Jamar starting dinner. They prepped the meal for me by chopping the onions, carrots, and celery. Mo is currently browning the sausage as well.

"I never thought I'd see the day you cooked something," I say. She's the queen of takeout.

She laughs. "It's actually not that bad. Jamar knows what he's doing, and you left your recipe up on the iPad, so really it was simple."

"Great, so I can go get freshened up, and you two will finish making dinner?" I ask.

Mo puts down the wooden spoon and holds up both hands. "No, I think I'm good. You're free to take over."

I laugh and finish cooking the meat. Then I stir in the vegetables. I add garlic, salt, and pepper. Next, I get the pasta started before adding the beans, diced tomatoes, chicken broth, and rosemary to the meat and vegetables. Once the pasta is cooked to al dente, I add it to the rest of the mixture.

The garlic bread takes minutes to prep. I slice the

large loaf of French bread down the middle. Then I spread olive oil on both halves. I liberally add garlic powder, seasoned salt, and black pepper. It only takes a few minutes to cook in the broiler, and once it's finished, I slice it into individual pieces and place them in a basket to serve.

"Cam, can you grab the parmesan cheese from the refrigerator? We're just about ready to eat."

"You got it," he says.

Mo pours the wine for us, and Jamar carries the glasses to the table.

"I brought cheesecake from Cup of Jo," Jamar says. "I hope that's okay, but with Robin and me closing up the place, I didn't know if I'd have time to grab dessert elsewhere."

"It's totally fine," Cam says. "And thank you for taking care of things at Cup of Jo for us." He claps Jamar on the back.

"Everyone sit," I say, bringing the big pot of pasta fagioli to the table and placing it on the hot plate in the center.

"That smells so good. I've barely eaten all day," Mo says.

"How is Wes doing?" I ask, grabbing the ladle and serving Cam first.

"He's feeling better, but he said he was going to stick to cereal for dinner just to be on the safe side. He said to tell everyone hello for him." She grabs two pieces of garlic bread before passing the basket to Jamar.

"I hate to jump right into things, but what were you able to find out about Sabrina Kincade?" I ask Mo.

"First, why did you have me look up those two people?" she asks.

I forgot she was swamped at work today. She probably hasn't heard about the murder yet. "Before I get into the details, I have to tell you both that Quentin's new boss at the station doesn't want outside help on cases."

"Why did Quentin come to you then?" Mo asks. "I'm assuming that's what happened."

"It is, but Chief Harvey can't know about it. Quentin's sort of in hot water after turning down the position of chief of police. Not with Harvey, of course. I'm sure he was happy about it since he got the job, but the commissioner isn't happy with Quentin. And now with Chief Harvey insisting no one at the BFPD works with consultants, it means everything we do has to stay on the down low."

Mo shrugs. "We're usually working behind Quentin's back, so that won't be so different."

"Well, if anyone asks, that's exactly what we're doing," I say.

Jamar shakes his head. "I don't get why you keep helping that man."

"It's not about him. Well…" I bob my head from side to side. "I do blame him for my need to figure out crimes, but I'm not doing it for him. I'm doing it for myself and for the victims."

"Understandable," Jamar says. "I'll admit I get a rush helping you out with the cases."

"Alright, then, fill us in," Mo says.

"I don't know much, but Sabrina Kincade was murdered at Fantasy Fitness. Her body was discovered this morning by one of the custodial crew, Logan Ross."

"Ah, the other name. Okay, I'm following," she says, dipping her garlic bread into the pasta fagioli.

"Well, Cam and I spoke with Logan today, and from what he told us, I'm assuming Sabrina was killed sometime last night after she finished work. She was seemingly heading to the showers when she was assaulted from behind."

Mo bobs her head. "From the pictures I saw of her online, she was a tough woman. Her muscles were huge."

"Yeah, she taught self-defense classes at the gym, too, so whoever attacked her knew it wouldn't be easy to subdue her."

"Do the police have a murder weapon?" Jamar asks.

I shake my head. "Quentin and I are both assuming it was a free weight, but they haven't found evidence yet. According to Logan Ross, he cleaned the weights before he found the body."

Mo gets on her phone. "Not a problem," she says. "The forensics team can use luminol or phenolphthalein to detect hemoglobin."

"Say what?" Jamar asks.

Mo laughs. "Sorry, I was reading from this site I found online. Basically, it's saying that even if someone tried to use bleach to scrub away signs of blood, the police can still detect the presence of blood on an object."

"Then they'll find the murder weapon," Jamar says.

"Knowing Quentin, they already have found it, and he's neglected to tell me." Or he thought since I assumed it was a free weight, confirming that suspicion wouldn't be all that helpful.

"The problem is that if both the killer and Logan Ross cleaned the murder weapon, there's probably no DNA on it to link back to the killer," Cam says.

"We definitely need to see the video footage from the gym Thursday night," I say. "They must have caught at least a glimpse of the killer."

"I doubt it," Mo says.

"What do you mean?" I narrow my eyes at her as I take another spoonful.

"You said this happened at Fantasy Fitness, right?" she asks.

"Yeah. Why?"

"We had that storm Thursday night. I heard lightning hit a transformer on Lake View. Isn't that the same road the gym is on?"

"Yeah, I think so," I say.

"Then I doubt they had power."

"Which means they had no cameras." I sigh.

"So much for this case being easy," Jamar says.

"When are they ever?" I ask.

CHAPTER FOUR

Cup of Jo is packed Saturday morning. Mickey has a crowd around his table, and even though he doesn't have much information about the current case since the media doesn't know anything other than Sabrina's name and the place where the body was found, he's spouting out theories left and right.

"I'll bet you it was one of her male clients who couldn't handle a woman having bigger muscles than he does," Mickey says.

Several heads bob in agreement.

"Are you saying you'd be threatened by a woman with larger muscles?" I ask Mickey.

He jerks his head back. "Me? No. I've never lifted a weight in my life. I mean I do manual labor, but I don't lift at the gym. I say good for any woman who gets herself into that kind of shape. It's a tough world out there. Everyone should be capable of protecting themselves."

"But she couldn't," Mrs. Marlow says. She doesn't look seventy years old, and she can verbally spar with the best of them, but she's a small woman. Definitely never into weight lifting.

"How does anyone defend themselves against an ambush from behind?" Erica Daniels, an art teacher at the high school asks. She's big into yoga, so the woman is pretty fit herself.

"Don't they teach that in self-defense classes?" Mickey asks. "You'd think since Sabrina taught self-defense, she'd have a way to defend herself in that situation."

"Want me to hit you over the head from behind and see how you defend yourself?" Mrs. Marlow asks, eliciting laughs from everyone around the table.

Mickey holds up both hands in front of him. "Okay, okay. I see your point."

Just then, Quentin walks into Cup of Jo.

"Maybe the good detective will have some news for us," Mickey says.

Quentin's been throwing the gossip mill some bones by talking loudly about a few things lately, so they've warmed up to him a bit. But since this case is supposed to be hush-hush, I know that won't happen this time.

"Hey, guys," I say, leaning toward the table. "I'm looking into this behind Quentin's back, so if you could avoid talking to him about the case, I'd appreciate it. If he knows you guys are discussing it, he'll assume it's because I'm investigating on my own."

Mickey winks at me. "We've got your back, Jo. You just keep us in the loop."

"Will do," I say. "I'll send Robin over with some refills too while I get rid of the detective." They buy my ruse, and I walk away with a smile on my face.

Robin is at the counter taking Quentin's order, but I tell her, "Could you get refills for Mickey's table? I'll help Detective Perry."

"Sure thing, Boss," she says, grabbing the pot of freshly brewed coffee and heading for the table.

"What can I get for you, Detective?" I ask.

"I'll take a large dark roast. I'm in a hurry. I have to interview a few employees from Fantasy Fitness this morning."

I nod and pour his dark roast. I cap the cup and slide it across the counter to him. "It's too bad about the storm killing the transformer and knocking out the power on Lake View Thursday night. I hope they've gotten it fixed by now," I say, trying to mask my hidden question of whether or not the camera feeds are useless to the case.

"Yeah, all the businesses on that road lost power," he confirms. "Things are up and running now, though."

"Well, good luck with your interviews. Can I get you anything else?"

"No." He hands me a ten-dollar bill.

Under the bill is a note, the yellow paper sticking out slightly. I discreetly pocket it before placing the money in the drawer and getting Quentin's change. "Here you go, Detective. Have a nice day." If anyone is watching too closely, they'd probably be suspicious since Quentin and I are never this cordial with each other.

He nods and walks out with this coffee. I turn and head for the kitchen. Cam is pulling more pastries out of the oven.

"Has the crowd died down at all?" he asks me. "I can't remember the last time I had to bake so much. It's like we can't keep the display case filled."

"It's still packed," I say, pulling the note from my pocket.

"What's that?" Cam asks after setting the tray aside to cool.

"Quentin slipped this to me when he paid for his coffee." I unfold the paper and read it aloud. "'Murder weapon was a fifteen-pound free weight. No video feed. No suspects.'"

"Sounds like no nothing," Cam says.

"Exactly. Still, I wonder why the killer chose the fifteen-pound weight," I say.

"You think the weight means something?" he asks.

"It might not, but it could. I mean a woman would probably need two hands to hit someone over the head with fifteen pounds."

"Maybe. Depends on the woman."

"True. But I think it might mean the killer is a man."

"If the gym wasn't closed for the day, I'd say it would be

difficult for a man to sneak into the women's locker room, but since it seems like Sabrina was the last one at the gym after closing, gender doesn't seem to factor into the equation, at least as far as locker room access is concerned."

"You're right. Sabrina was strong, so it would make more sense that the killer would be male. Of course, an attack from behind would be a surprise, so maybe the killer's size doesn't matter." We're talking in circles. No wonder the police have nothing. There are too many possibilities.

"What's the plan then?" Cam asks, wiping down the island where he prepares the baked goods.

"I wish I knew." I give him a small smile before leaving the kitchen.

Mo and Wes walk into Cup of Jo, holding hands. I smile at them.

"Hey, Wes, glad to see you're feeling better."

"Yeah, sorry I had to miss dinner last night. I heard it was delicious." He smiles at Mo before turning back to me.

"No problem. I was worried you both might be sick today when I didn't see you before work this morning." One or both of them usually stop in for their morning coffee and baked goods before starting their workdays.

"I got an early jump on my workday to catch up on stuff from yesterday," Wes says.

"And I had coffee waiting for me on my desk," Mo adds.

I cock my head. "Then you were here, and I missed you somehow."

Wes turns about six shades of red as he drags his free hand through his hair. "Not exactly. I had to pick up my truck from the mechanic on Lake View this morning, and I sort of grabbed coffee from the coffee truck." He couldn't look guiltier.

I laugh. "It's fine. I know Cup of Jo isn't the only place in town to get a decent cup of coffee."

"Actually, the coffee wasn't very good. Very watered down," Wes says.

"You don't have to say that. I'm really fine with it, Wes."

"I told you Jo wouldn't care," Mo says. "I'm starving. What does Cam recommend this morning?"

"I'd go with the banana hazelnut bread. It has an espresso glaze on top, and it's to die for. Customers have been raving about it. Cam's already made four loaves this morning."

"We'll take two huge slices," Mo says.

"I'll give you four, just to be on the safe side." I grab a to-go box and prepare the order.

Mo lets go of Wes's hand to lean on the counter. "I found out some things for you last night. I'll email them to you. It's stuff you might want to look into." She keeps her voice low to avoid drawing attention.

"Good because I didn't really know where to start today."

Mo nods, and customers line up behind her, so she

says, "I think we'll take two hazelnut coffees this morning to go with the banana hazelnut bread." She stands up tall again.

"You got it." I finish getting them settled and motion for Robin to come relieve me at the register before I head to the kitchen to check for Mo's email. Since she and Wes work in the office building directly across the street, it will take them about two minutes to get there. I should have Mo's email in no time.

"Hey," Cam says, pulling muffins from a tray and placing them on the cooling rack. "Did I see Mo and Wes out there?" He peers through the kitchen window.

"You did, but they're gone now."

"How's Wes doing?"

"Much better." I open my email on my phone.

"You seem distracted. What's up?"

"Mo is emailing me what she found out about Sabrina Kincade."

"Ah." Cam bobs his head. "I'll be finished here soon if we need to head out to talk to anyone."

I refresh my inbox for the third time, and Mo's email pops up. "Got it." I click on it. "Okay, so Sabrina wasn't married. She had a roommate, a woman named Jade Summers. They shared a house on Ivy Way."

"What are the odds the roommate will be home during the day?" Cam asks.

"Not likely. Mo didn't find a place of work for her either." It could be a waste of time going to the house if Jade isn't home.

"Did she give you anyone else to look into?" Cam asks, walking over to look at the email with me.

"No, it just says she's worked at the gym for the past two years as a fitness instructor."

"Okay, so our options are stay here and not work on the case, or go to the house and hope we're lucky enough to find Sabrina's roommate at home."

He's right. Something is better than nothing. If we stay, we'll definitely get nowhere. "I'll drive," I say.

Cam removes his apron, which is white with lace because it belonged to his grandmother, who happens to be the one who taught him to bake.

We let Robin and Jamar know we're leaving for a bit.

"We've got this," Jamar says, dipping Mrs. Marlow.

"We're going to have to take out extra insurance in case Jamar drops any of our customers and breaks their hips," I tell Cam as we get into my car.

He laughs. "That might not be a bad idea. There's really no stopping him, not with the way the customers eat up his antics. And the tip mug is always overflowing."

I pull out of my parking spot and onto Main Street. "Yeah, I bet that coffee truck doesn't have entertainment like that."

"What coffee truck?" Cam asks.

"Oh, Wes mentioned he had to pick up his truck this morning at the shop on Lake View. There's a coffee truck on that road."

"Ah." Cam bobs his head. "He cheated on Cup of Jo. I thought he looked pained when I saw him through the window. Now, I understand his expression was one of guilt."

"I'm not upset about it. Wes comes to Cup of Jo every day."

"And he and Mo don't usually pay," Cam says.

"Exactly, so I know I won't lose him to this coffee truck that actually takes his money," I joke.

Sabrina and Jade's home is a white cape cod with a wraparound front porch. It's really cute with decorations on the porch and front door. Either Sabrina or Jade takes great care of the place—at least the outside.

I park in the driveway, and we ring the doorbell. To my surprise, a man answers the door. He's wearing lounge pants and no shirt, exposing his very hairy chest.

"Can I help you?" he asks us, reaching up and placing his hand high up on the door, giving me a clear view of his armpit hair.

"I'm sorry. Maybe we have the wrong house. We're looking for Jade Summers," I say.

"This is her place. She's at work, though."

"Oh, and who might you be?" I ask, guessing he's Jade's boyfriend.

"Who's asking?"

"I'm Joanna Coffee, and this is Camden Turner. We own Cup of Jo on Main Street."

He bobs his head. "I like your cheesecake."

"Thank you," Cam says.

"Do you know what time Jade will be home?" I ask.

"She works at the convenience store on Second

Street. She's usually home by lunchtime since she works the early morning shift."

"Could we possibly wait for her?" Cam asks.

"What for?" the man asks.

"We'd like to talk to her about Sabrina Kincade," I say.

"I can tell you about Sabrina," the man says. "I knew her better than Jade did." The expression on his face says it all. This man had a thing for his girlfriend's roommate.

Well, that's interesting. I wonder if Jade knew about it, because that could certainly be motive for murder.

CHAPTER FIVE

Cam and I exchange a look as the man lets us into the house. Mo didn't mention this guy in her email, so I still have no idea what his name is.

"I'm sorry, but I didn't catch your name," I say.

"Hudson Moon." He brings us into the living room and motions to the couch.

Cam and I sit side by side on the sectional sofa, and Hudson sits on the love seat.

"What can you tell us about Sabrina?" Cam asks.

Hudson motions between us. "How do you two know her?"

"We don't really," I say. "We heard about her murder."

Hudson furrows his brow. "And what? You decided you're smarter than the cops and could figure out who did it before them?"

I bob one shoulder. "Pretty much." My tone has a teasing quality to it, and it makes Hudson laugh.

"You're probably right. I heard some lady in town has solved a few murders before those bozos at the BFPD."

I raise my hand ever so slightly. "That lady would be me."

Hudson laughs. "No doubt! Do you want my help or something?"

"Anything you could tell us about Sabrina Kincade would be helpful," I say.

Hudson leans back on the love seat, extending his right arm across the back cushion. "Okay, well she's my girlfriend's roommate. Sabrina bought the house when she started working at that gym, but mortgages are expensive, so she decided she needed a roommate."

"And she asked Jade to move in with her?" Cam asks.

"Nah. Jade and Sabrina didn't know each other. Jade answered the ad Sabrina put out. Jade had just moved to Bennett Falls, so she needed a place to live. Have you seen some of the apartments for rent here?" He shakes his head and scoffs. "Mine is awful. That's why I spend most of my time here."

"Will you move in now that Sabrina is gone?" I ask.

"Can't. The place is in Sabrina's name. I'm not sure what's going to happen to it. I guess Jade can try to buy it from the bank since Sabrina didn't have any family left, but who knows?"

"Sabrina doesn't have any living relatives?" I ask.

46

"Not that she knows of. She was a foster kid. She was pretty proud of the fact that despite being juggled from one foster home to another, she turned out alright. Got herself a job, bought this house…" He flips his hand, motioning to the room.

"Do you know how she managed to afford this place?" I ask.

"Yeah, she got into an accident about two years ago. She won some money in a small claims court."

"What kind of accident?" Cam asks, leaning forward and resting his forearms on his knees.

"She was living in a tiny apartment at the time. Her neighbor got into a fight with her man and was tossing his stuff out the window. Sabrina was coming home from work, and she got hit with an alarm clock or something. Knocked her out cold."

"She sued?" I ask.

He bobs his head. "She told me she never liked her neighbor, and the concussion she got made her miss work for a few days. The judge granted her twelve thousand dollars, believe it or not."

"Wow." My eyes widen.

"Yeah. That's the maximum for small claims in Pennsylvania. At least, that's what Sabrina told me. I think the judge liked her. She was a beautiful woman." He looks up, and I'm pretty sure he's picturing her in his mind.

"I'm assuming she used the money as a down payment on this house," Cam says.

"Sort of. She placed a bet on a horse race and won

big. She'd never bet on anything before in her life, but she told me she had this dream about a horse, and then she saw the announcement of the race on TV. She thought it was a sign or something. I thought she was crazy because she put the whole twelve grand on the horse. She won, though. Turned that twelve grand into over one hundred thousand, and she got this house."

"That's an incredible story," I say.

"Yeah, she later remembered that she saw the same advertisement for the race the night before when she fell asleep." Hudson laughs. "So really it wasn't a sign that she dreamed about the horse. It was just the last thing on her mind before going to bed."

She could have lost everything. Of course, she did wind up losing everything considering she was murdered.

The front door opens. "Hudson, I'm home," a woman calls.

"In here, babe. We have company," Hudson says, not bothering to get up.

The woman walks into the room and slings her purse onto the armchair. "Who are they?" she asks Hudson.

He looks at us, clearly having forgotten our names.

Cam stands up and extends his hand. "I'm Camden Turner, and this is my girlfriend, Joanna Coffee. You must be Jade."

She shakes his hand. "Yeah, that's me."

"We're looking into your roommate's murder," I say as Cam retakes his seat beside me.

"Oh." Jade sits next to Hudson on the love seat.

"Crazy, right? I mean Sabrina was a tough cookie. You didn't mess with muscles like she had."

Someone did.

"You make it sound like she was a bodybuilder," Hudson says. "She wasn't. Yeah, she was fit. Really fit." The way he says it makes Jade smack his chest. Hard if the slapping sound is any indication. "What?" Hudson says. "It's true. She took care of herself."

"Yeah, but you don't have to be so obvious about your crush on her. I'm sitting right here." Jade crosses her arms.

Okay, so Jade is clearly jealous of Sabrina. Or she used to be.

"Jade, what can you tell us about Sabrina?" I ask.

She bobs her shoulders. "Not much. I've only known her for about two years. She kept to herself. She was either working at the gym or working out at the gym, so she was there practically twenty-four seven."

"Do you know who her close friends were?" I ask.

Jade's face falls. "She didn't really have any. She was always working. She came home to sleep, so I can't say I really knew her either."

"What about you, Hudson?" Cam asks.

Jade turns to face Hudson. "What are you telling these people? You didn't know Sabrina any better than I did."

"Well, that's not true. I'd talk to her in the mornings when you were at work." Hudson turns to us. "Sabrina didn't work in the mornings. She worked afternoons and evenings."

I'm getting the impression Hudson doesn't work at all. He's a freeloader here, living off of Jade while pining over her roommate. Poor Jade.

"What do you do, Hudson?" Cam asks.

Hudson clears his throat. "I'm currently between jobs."

"He got hurt at a job site. Huds works in construction."

Huds? That's an unfortunate nickname.

"Doc says I need to take it easy for a few months so my back can get better."

It's clear taking it easy means sitting on the couch and drinking beer. At least, I'm assuming his belly came to look like that from drinking.

"Sabrina never mentioned any friends to you?" I ask Hudson.

"Nah. She'd sometimes talk about her clients or her boss. She didn't like her boss. Said the guy was a jerk."

"But she never thought about quitting?" I ask.

"She loved her job. She said she was used to men hitting on her. Besides, she took over after some woman got pregnant and left on maternity leave. Sabrina was afraid she'd lose her job if the woman wanted to come back, so she was careful not to cause any trouble at work. She wanted to convince her boss to keep her over the other woman. She never mentioned the harassment to anyone but me."

"Wait." Cam holds up a hand. "Are you saying her boss was sexually harassing her?"

I'd be surprised she didn't bring a lawsuit against him for that considering she sued her former roommate and won.

"No, he didn't harass her. He asked her out a few times. She said no. He stopped, but then he gave her a hard time about everything. You know, like he held a grudge." Hudson pulls at a string on the back of the couch. "I offered to talk to him for her, but she said it wasn't necessary."

Jade bursts out laughing. "What were you going to do? Sabrina was stronger than you, especially considering your back is injured."

I'm not sure his back is injured. I haven't noticed him showing any signs of being in discomfort. And the way he's twisting now would probably be painful if he did have a back injury. He's playing Jade for a fool.

"I was planning to talk to the guy, man to man."

Jade rolls her eyes. "Anyway, I have no idea what's going to happen now. The house is in Sabrina's name. I'm sure I'll have to move out once the bank takes it over."

Jade might have been jealous that Hudson was into Sabrina, but I can't see her killing Sabrina when it means losing this house. Still, she doesn't seem the least bit broken up over the fact that her roommate is dead. They clearly weren't close at all.

"We should probably get going," I say, standing up. "Thank you both for talking to us."

"You're a lot friendlier than that detective." Jade shakes her head and walks us to the front door. Hudson doesn't even bother to get up off the love seat.

"Babe, grab me a beer after you walk them out," he calls.

Jade rolls her eyes again. Part of me wants to ask her what she's doing with a guy like him, but it's really none of my business.

"Thanks again for talking to us," I say.

Jade leans her head against the front door. "Look, I didn't know Sabrina well, but I am sorry this happened to her. I hope you find the person who killed her."

She seems genuine, but I can't stop myself from saying, "I intend to," just to gauge her reaction.

She nods and closes the door.

Cam places his hand on my lower back as we walk to my car. "Think either one of them could have done it?"

"My gut says no."

"How about some lunch?" Cam asks.

My stomach growls in response. "Sounds good."

We decide on the pizza place right on Lake View. It's across the street from the gym, which still looks closed. We take a table outside since it's a nice day. The waiter brings us some lemonade while we wait for the calzone we ordered to share.

"There's the coffee truck," I say, lifting one finger off my lemonade to point in the direction. It's nothing fancy, not that you expect a food truck to be fancy. It's white—well, dingy white. There's a big window on the side. One of those latch types that you swing upward and hold in place with a bar. "Seriously, someone could really get injured if that bar let go."

Cam laughs. "You are totally intimidated by a coffee truck."

"I bet he doesn't even sell food."

"Shouldn't I be the one worried about the food? That is my domain at Cup of Jo." Cam sips his lemonade.

"Why does this bother me so much?" I ask. "He's a fellow entrepreneur. I should be supportive. It's not like he parked his truck in front of Cup of Jo."

Cam puts down his drink. "You better hope he never does. I could see one of our regulars offing the guy, and you getting blamed."

"Don't even kid about that. I love how loyal our regulars are, but I wouldn't put it past them to do something like that."

"Yeah and then attack Quentin when he accused you of the murder."

"Here's your calzone and two plates," the waiter says, placing the calzone in the center of the table. It smells delicious.

"Hey, do you happen to know how long that coffee truck has been here?" I ask the waiter.

He looks across the street at the truck and lets out a long breath before saying, "I think a few months now. Why?"

"I'm just curious," I say.

"We own Cup of Jo on Main Street," Cam tells him.

"Oh." The waiter smiles. "I knew I recognized you guys. I was there last week. I had some really great peach pie and the best cappuccino of my life."

I have a feeling the waiter sensed my jealousy and is trying to appease me, but I thank him all the same. When he walks away, I ask Cam, "Am I really that bad?"

He bobs his head. "Sorry, but yes." He cuts the calzone in two and places one half on my plate.

The waiter returns with two extra bowls of marinara sauce. "Customers tend to request extra, so I thought I'd bring it to you right away."

"Thank you." I cut off a bite of calzone and dip it into the sauce. My eyes widen, and I cover my mouth with a hand. "This is easily the best sauce I've ever had."

Cam tries it and says, "Agreed. It's fantastic."

The waiter smiles and walks away.

"They should bottle this stuff," I say, indulging in some more.

We continue eating, people watching at the same time. A woman pushing a baby stroller approaches the coffee truck. The man that sticks his head through the window has graying hair and big muscles. He's also wearing what appears to be a dog tag around his neck.

"I bet he'd be more than capable of attacking a woman as fit as Sabrina Kincade."

"Jo," Cam says, "you can't go accusing the guy because he's our competition."

"Seriously, though. Look at his muscles. And I think he's wearing a dog tag. If he's a vet, he'd be fit and could have combat training."

Cam reaches for my hand. "You need to let this go."

"I will. After we question him."

Cam releases my hand and cocks his head.

"I'm serious. His truck is right outside the gym. I'm willing to bet Sabrina has gotten coffee from him."

"Fine, I'll give you that one, but that doesn't mean anything."

He could have waited inside his coffee truck, murdered Sabrina, and then driven off without anyone being the wiser. I don't say that out loud, though, because Cam will chalk it up to me being bitter. Maybe I am, but with no suspects at the moment, I'm not willing to rule out anyone.

"It's worth seeing what he knows," I say.

Cam sighs. "Okay, we'll talk to him after we finish eating. Maybe then you'll stop accusing the poor guy of things."

Maybe. Or maybe he'll move into the position of my prime suspect in Sabrina's murder.

CHAPTER SIX

Cam and I finish every last bite of the calzone and every drop of marinara. I'm so stuffed but so satisfied at the same time. We place a nice tip on the table and leave with every intention of coming back to try the other menu items.

We walk across the street to the coffee truck.

"You know we'll have to order something," Cam says.

"Wes said the coffee wasn't very good."

Cam laughs. "Hmm, your sister's boyfriend said you make better coffee than this coffee truck guy? Shocking." He bumps his shoulder into mine.

"Keep it up, Camden Turner, and I'll tell Mickey you're not being very nice to me." Mickey will have all my other customers giving Cam a hard time in a matter of seconds.

"Oh, I see how it is. You know the residents of this town love you."

"The ones who know me, at least." When Cam tried to open his own place, it failed, mostly because of me. I had no idea at the time that people were avoiding Cam's Kitchen because they were upset he wasn't selling his baked goods at Cup of Jo anymore. Even though I was the one who encouraged Cam to open his own place, people thought he'd betrayed me in some way. Now that Cam and I have joined forces, everyone loves him again. Bennett Falls is a strange little town.

There's no line at the coffee truck, so Cam rings the orange bell set out on the windowsill. Or is it a counter?

The same man we saw earlier walks up to the window. "What can I get for you?" he asks us with a smile.

I look at the small menu board. It's basically a piece of white paper with coffee drinks scribbled on it. "I'll take an Americano," I say, curious if he waters it down more than it's supposed to be. An Americano is basically an espresso that's diluted with water to taste more like regular coffee.

"Sure thing. And for you?" He turns to Cam.

"I'll take an espresso."

The man taps the metal counter. "Coming right up."

He turns around and brews the espresso.

"I just heard about you," I say. "You must be new to the area."

"I moved here about three months ago," the man says over his shoulder.

"What made you decide on this location for your truck?"

"There's already this great coffee place on Main Street. Most people in town go there. I think it's called Cup of Jo."

I swallow hard. Do I tell him we own it? I choose to remain silent for now, and Cam does the same.

"I figured I didn't want to be too close to that place since it was already established."

"Have you been there?" I can't help asking. Maybe Cam and I were out when this guy came in. I need to know if he checked out his competition.

"I tried twice. The place was packed both times. This guy was dancing around with the customers. It looked like a lot of fun, but I decided not to go in."

"Why's that?" I ask.

"Well, I can't afford to have a place like that. I bought this truck for next to nothing, and I have one espresso machine. You can't do much with that."

Cam looks at me, and I can't help but feel a little guilty. Maybe I should come clean.

The guy hands us our drinks, and Cam gives him a twenty-dollar bill. As the guy gets Cam's change, I sip my Americano. It's just right.

"This is good," I say.

"Thanks." The man hands Cam his change.

"I'm Joanna Coffee. I own Cup of Jo along with Cam here." I dip my head in Cam's direction, and he smiles at me.

"Camden Turner," he tells the man.

"Oh." The man pauses, clearly blindsided. "I'm Mac. Well, Gerald MacLean, but everyone calls me Mac."

"Nice to meet you, Mac."

He squints at us. "I have to ask. If you own a great place like that, why are you buying coffee from me? Are you scouting out my truck?"

"Actually, we're looking into a murder that happened at the gym right there Thursday night," I say. "We thought since your truck is here, you might have seen something."

"I close up for the night at seven. The cops were here Friday morning. I had to shut down because no one could get near the place. They had the entire road blocked off."

"Sorry to hear that," I say because I'm sure it was a financial hit for him, and if he really didn't have anything to do with the murder, then that's unfortunate.

"Do you keep your truck here all the time?" I ask. If it's mobile, he could have moved it to another location on Friday.

"Yeah, I do. It doesn't actually run. I mean I have electric and all that, but the engine needs to be repaired, and I don't exactly have the money to fix it right now." His cheeks turn red, and he avoids our gaze.

"We're curious if you knew Sabrina Kincade," I say, sensing he doesn't want to talk about his problems.

"Knew?" Mac raises his head, a questioning look on

his face. "Are you saying…? Is she the one who…?" He turns toward the gym.

"Yes, she was. It seems like you did know her. I'm sorry for your loss," I say.

Mac blinks a few times. "This is silly. I mean I barely knew her. She was one of my regulars, though. She stopped by every day for an Americano on her way to work."

How odd that I happened to be serving Americanos the day her body was discovered, and that was her drink of choice.

Mac offers a small, sad smile. "I remember the first time she stopped here. She didn't know what to order. She said everyone she knew loved espresso, but she found it to be too strong. That's when I told her about Americanos. I told her they taste a lot like regular coffee because they're watered down espressos."

I hold up mine. "It's delicious. I can see why she liked it enough to order it every day."

"You're kind. I'll have to stop in Cup of Jo sometime and try one of yours."

"It's ironic, but Americanos were my special on Friday."

Mac bobs his head. "I think Sabrina would have liked that."

"I'm guessing you talked to her every day then," Cam says.

"Yeah, I'm sure you guys know what it's like when you have regular customers. Every day you learn a little more about them." He blinks a few times as if trying to ward off tears.

"We do know," Cam says.

"Did Sabrina mention having trouble at work or with anyone in her personal life?" I ask.

"No, and I'd remember. I only have two regular clients, Sabrina and Erin. Erin comes here twice a day with her son. She's divorced. Her husband left her right after the baby was born. She watches the boy while he works during the day, and then they hand him off in the evening. Weird situation if you ask me."

This other woman really isn't my concern right now. "So Sabrina wasn't the type to talk about her problems, I'm guessing."

Mac cocks his head at me. "You're really trying to figure out who killed her, huh?"

"Don't you want to know?" I ask.

"Of course. But then again, if I found the guy responsible, I'd probably do something stupid."

I don't know Mac, so I can't tell if he's putting on a good show or not. It's possible he did grow to care about Sabrina since he's hurting for business and new to town. But it's also possible he's trying to throw us off.

"Was she ever with anyone when she stopped here for her coffee?" I ask, trying to get him to redirect to my questions.

"No, she was always alone. I thought that was weird because she was a nice lady. Very friendly. She always struck up conversations with me, and I'm not delusional enough to believe it was because she was interested in getting romantically involved with me. She was a beautiful woman. She could do much better than me. Plus, I have about fifteen years on her. Or rather, I had."

"What did she talk to you about?" I ask, finishing my Americano and tossing my empty cup into the trash can beside the coffee truck.

"Everything and anything. You know, the weather, baseball games—she was a Phillies fan—TV shows she watched the night before."

That could mean she didn't have much of a social life since there's no mention of friends. That fits with what Sabrina's roommate told us about her. "Did she tell you about the horse racing bet she won?" I ask.

Mac scrunches his forehead. "Horse racing? No, she never mentioned that. Was she a gambler? I didn't get that impression from her."

"Not really, but apparently she placed one bet on a horse and won big. She bought a house with the winnings, which was fortuitous because she had a tough childhood and probably wouldn't have been able to afford a house otherwise."

Mac nods. "She did have this air about her, and she'd get this far-off look sometimes. I sort of figured she had a rough past. I didn't ask about it because she never volunteered even a hint. I figured she'd bring it up if she wanted to, but then again, I was nothing more than the guy who served her coffee. Why would she confide in me?"

I wonder if that upset him, that she wouldn't open up when he could tell there was a story there.

"Anyway, it's awful that she's gone," Mac says. "Here I was thinking the gym being closed and my sales being affected by it was the worst thing that was going to happen to me today."

He still knew there was a murder the day before, even if he didn't know it was Sabrina—which I'm not ruling out at this point because I don't know how much I can trust this man—and his concern is a slow day? That lack of empathy for human life doesn't seem to fit the mourning individual he's trying to portray. Something is off about this guy.

"Well, I hope things pick up for you soon," I say. "Cam, we should get going. Jamar and Robin probably need us by now."

Cam says goodbye to Mac and then extends his elbow to me as we walk back to my car. "What was that about? You know as well as I do that Robin and Jamar are fine without us."

"Something about that guy isn't sitting well with me," I say.

"Yeah, the fact that he has a coffee truck in your town."

I stop at the driver's side door of my Accord. "What if that's just one tick in the negative column? What if there's a much bigger reason to not like this guy?"

Mo slaps her open palm against my kitchen table. "I can totally see you giving that guy a hard time! Did you flash your invisible badge and threaten to lock him up if he didn't start talking?"

"This isn't funny. For all we know, he did kill Sabrina. He had the opportunity."

"But no motive. She was a customer of his. If anything, killing her would lose business for him."

"Whatever." I flip a hand in the air.

"I can't believe you can't handle a little competition. I mean you opened a coffee shop when Mom and Dad have one in the next town. They didn't freak out over it."

"We have different clientele. Arameda is more old-school. They still have mailboxes on the corners." Even my parents' coffee shop, Time For Coffee, looks stuck in the past, which is actually a source of conflict for my parents at the moment. Dad wants to update the place, but Mom loves the charm of it. "Can you picture Cup of Jo's clientele in there?" I shake my head.

Mo doesn't argue that point.

"And he went back to work as if nothing happened," I say, launching right back into my reasoning for Mac being the top suspect on our list.

"Who?" Wes asks.

"Mac, the coffee truck guy. He returned to the scene of the crime, and you know what that means." I fork a bite of chicken Caesar salad into my mouth.

"I don't know why people say the killer always returns to the scene of the crime," Mo says. "If I ever committed a crime, I'd get as far away from the crime scene as possible. It's just not smart to stick around and hope you don't get caught."

"Yeah, but running would make you look guilty," Wes says.

"I've seen shows where the killer actually joins the search for a missing person because they want to look innocent. More than once on those shows, it was even the killer who discovered the body." Quentin got me into those shows when we dated, and while I don't watch a whole lot of television, I will throw on a show like that when I'm lounging around.

"Well, he'd know exactly where the body was, so it would be easy to find it, right?" Mo asks.

Wes bobs his head and sips his margarita. "Yeah, and he comes across looking like the hero."

"Wes is right," I say.

Mo laughs. "Then I'm surprised we all haven't been accused of murder.

"I have. Multiple times, and maybe Wes's theory is the reason why." I put down my fork and push my plate away. "I'm stuffed."

"Me, too, but the conversation is entertaining, so I keep eating," Jamar says.

"You've been very quiet," I say. "No thoughts on any of this?"

Jamar wipes his mouth on a napkin. "You're my boss. I'm not about to tell you you're wrong about this. But,

I'm not about to accuse this guy Mac of anything yet either."

"Fair enough, I suppose."

"What's the plan for tomorrow?" Mo asks, beginning to clear the table.

"I'm not sure yet. I guess I need to get into the gym and talk to Sabrina's boss and coworkers, but I'm not sure when it's reopening to the public."

"You also can't get into that gym without a membership or being accompanied by someone with a membership," Wes says.

"I don't suppose you have one, do you?" I ask. Wes is in good shape, but then again so is Cam, and he doesn't go to the gym. He's on a coffee and baked goods diet, which should equate to a very different figure than the one he has. He must have an exceptional metabolism.

"Sorry, can't help you there," Wes says.

"You could always pretend you want to get a membership," Mo suggests, loading the rest of the dishes into the dishwasher.

Wes shakes his head and leans against the kitchen counter. "They don't allow that there. I know a guy who asked if he could tour the place because he was thinking of joining, and they told him they have a strict policy against that. They have videos and brochures you can look at. That's it."

Cam starts brewing coffee for our dessert. "I bet a lot of people try to con their way into getting free workouts by claiming to want a trial before committing to a membership. The owners of the gym probably got fed up with those people and banned the practice at all."

"A classic case of a few people ruining things for everyone," Jamar says, putting the flourless chocolate cake on the table.

That means I can't even get inside the gym when they do reopen unless I'm willing to fork over a ton of money for a membership I'll never use. "Think Quentin will foot the bill for a gym membership for me?" I ask.

Everyone laughs.

I'm totally screwed.

CHAPTER SEVEN

Sunday morning, I still don't know what to do. I'm tempted to put out a tip jar to raise money for the gym membership. I figure quite a few of my regulars would contribute to the fund if they thought it was to go behind Quentin's back and solve this case. Little do they know this charade of not working with Quentin is helping him keep his job. I'm not sure how they'd feel about that. They were getting along with him until we created this ruse that I'm once again investigating without Quentin knowing.

It's not that I can't afford the gym membership myself. Money isn't that tight. However, I did take out a loan when I opened Cup of Jo, and Cam and I have to pay Jamar and Robin, so while business is good, we aren't rolling in dough yet. Hopefully, we will be one day. A little while back, I came into an inheritance from a local investor. I didn't really know the man, although I solved his murder. I had great motivation, considering I'd just moved back to town and Quentin accused me of the murder. I didn't keep that inheritance check, though. I gave it to Jamar's friend Lance, who is now my friend as well, because he was opening his own restaurant at the time and really needed the money more than I did. S.C. Tunney's is an upscale restaurant in Highland Hills, which is about twenty minutes from here. Every time I go there and see Lance thriving, it makes me smile.

"Why do you look so happy?" Mo asks, walking up to the register.

"Why are you back again so soon this morning?" I ask her since she's already been to Cup of Jo for her usual morning coffee and sugar fix.

"I have a meeting to go to across town. It's with a new prospective client." Mo works in social media advertising. She's amazingly good at her job, so I have no doubt she'll land this client. "Let me guess. You want to show up with some coffee and baked goods to sweeten the deal."

"Hey, I created your Cup of Jo logo, didn't I? It will allow the client to see my work in action. You guys are doing well here, so I'm sure it will impress them."

"Why not take them to S.C. Tunney's? Lance is a pretty big success story as well."

"True, but most of the work I did for Lance was pro bono back when he couldn't afford to pay me. My company didn't have a hand in much of it, although Lance is officially one of our clients now."

"I think it still wouldn't hurt to drop the name of the restaurant then."

She cocks her head as she thinks about it. "Maybe you're right. I'm still bringing coffee and pastries, though. What do you recommend?"

I scan the display case. "Well, there's an assortment of biscotti this morning: almond, hazelnut, cappuccino, orange, walnut, pecan, chocolate dipped—"

Mo holds up a hand to stop me. "Okay, wow. I guess Cam was on a biscotti kick this morning. I'll take a box with a few of each."

"You got it. What kind of coffee?"

"How about four Americanos? I don't want to bring regular coffee because it sounds too blah, but I don't want to assume what people like. I figure the Americano is a safe choice, right?"

"Sure. It sounds fancier than it actually is." I get to work filling the pastry box and set it on the counter. Then I make four Americanos, cap the cups, and place them in a drink caddy.

Mo pulls out a credit card, which is odd because I never charge her. "It's the company card," she says. "This is for a business deal."

I take the card. "I see. I have no problem charging it then." I ring up the order, and Mo even adds a tip. "Oh, here. Take some chocolate straws." I grab a few from the container next to the register and place them between the drinks in the caddy.

"Thanks. Wish me luck."

"You don't need luck. You're Mo Coffee."

We both crack up when I say it. Why our parents gave us such ridiculous names, we'll never know. I mean naming your second child Mo Coffee? More coffee since she's the second born. I can't even attempt to understand some things when it comes to Mom and Dad. They're lucky we love them.

At least the name made Mo smile and hopefully eased her nerves before the meeting. My own smile fades when Samantha walks into Cup of Jo, holding a small bouquet of flowers. Is she delivering to one of my customers? I watch as she walks up to the counter and places the bouquet next to the register. "These are for you from Quentin," she says with a sniffle.

"What? Why?" I couldn't be more confused as I stare at the bouquet like it's a ticking time bomb.

"He just told me to give them to you." In a manner that's as un-Samantha-like as it gets, she turns and walks away without another word.

"Quentin sent you flowers?" Cam asks, a little too loudly, drawing the attention of everyone in Cup of Jo. I didn't even see him come out of the kitchen, but he's holding a tray of fresh blueberry muffins.

Why would Quentin give me flowers, and why would he have his wife deliver them? That's going to get people talking.

Mickey stands up from his table and walks over to me. "What's going on here, Jo? He motions to the bouquet. "Are those really from Quentin? Did I hear Sam correctly?"

"Um..." My gaze spans the coffee shop, taking in every inch of the space and all the peering eyes as well. I need to think quickly before this escalates out of control. "I think it's a peace offering or even a poorly veiled threat." I wag a finger in the air. "It's probably that one. You know. A warning to stay away from his case." I give Cam the side eye, hoping he'll play along until I can figure out what's really going on.

Cam bobs his head. "That would be just like Quentin."

Mickey nods and crosses his arms. "Yeah, I think you're on to something there. You let me know if he threatens you with anything else. We've got your back, Jo."

I almost feel guilty for making everyone think Quentin is being a jerk when he just started to regain a shred of their respect. This is going to put him back at square one, but it's still better than Quentin losing his job over asking for my help, right? It has to be. I pick up the bouquet. "I'm dumping these in the kitchen garbage. I don't even want to look at them."

"I'll help you," Cam says, walking with me.

As soon as we're in the kitchen with the door closed, Cam turns to me with upturned palms. "What is this really about?"

I shrug. "I have no idea, but he must be trying to tell me something, right? First, it was the note under the ten-dollar bill, and now this. I mean there's no other explanation that I can see."

"There's no card?" he asks.

"I didn't even look since Samantha told me the flowers were from Quentin. How did he even get her to deliver them without her questioning him or even me about it? She handed them to me and left."

"That was really weird. Quentin must be up to something, but to get Samantha on board with the plan must have taken a lot of work on his end."

"Agreed." I start moving aside the petals of the colorful flowers until I find a small plastic card holder with an envelope attached. I remove the envelope and peer inside it. It doesn't contain a card at all. "It's Samantha's gym membership to Fantasy Fitness."

Cam's brow furrows as he stares at the ID badge in my hand. "Do you think she put it in there by mistake? She's been very scatterbrained lately. I mean more than usual."

I only have to think about it for a moment. "No. I think this is Quentin's way of telling me the gym is open to the public, and I need to go talk to some people there. You know, Sabrina's coworkers, clients, and anyone else who was at the gym Thursday night."

"That means he knows about the membership restrictions at the gym, and he wants you to pretend to be Samantha." Cam reaches for the card. "Jo, her picture is on the ID card. How are you going to pull this off?"

I've never been to the gym, but that doesn't mean

there's no chance of anyone there not recognizing me. Bennett Falls is a small town. Most people know who I am, either because they're friends with me or my parents or they've been to Cup of Jo. This won't be easy at all.

"Maybe I only need the card to get in. I'm pretty sure by the looks of this that they have a keycard entry system. I'll bet no one even asks to see the ID."

"Let's hope so," Cam says, "because no offense, but I don't think you'd make a good blond." He cracks a smile.

"Oh, and I'd pull off the rest of Samantha's attributes no problem?" I ask. Not to mention she's pregnant. I'm not about to fake that.

"Not for a second," Cam says, and then he kisses the side of my head. "And I'm very thankful for that."

"I wish you could come with me," I say, realizing I'm going to have to do this alone since Quentin didn't send an ID badge for Cam.

Cam leans against the island where he prepares the food. "How did that part of this plan elude me until now? I don't like the idea of you going there on your own."

"I could maybe get you in as a guest, but then I'm sure they'll ask for my name and information and insist on seeing my membership badge." Things would go south before we got to talk to anyone important to the case.

"No. It's too risky. You're going to have to go on your own."

"I'm sorry. I hate this as much as you do." I rub my hand up and down his left arm.

"Just promise me——"

"I'll be careful."

Cam smirks. "Well, that too, but I was going to say promise me you won't go accusing Mac, the coffee truck guy, of killing Sabrina Kincade."

I don't like lying in general, but I especially hate to lie to Cam, so I shrug one shoulder instead of responding.

Even though the gym is open again, there aren't many cars out front, and there's not a single soul at the coffee truck. I hate to admit I catch myself smiling at that fact. I'm not sure what's wrong with me. I'm not the super jealous type, so why does this coffee truck get me so worked up? Before I realize what I'm doing, I'm standing in front of the window of Mac's truck.

"Morning, Jo," he says. "I didn't expect to see you again."

Did he sense my feelings for him?

"I'm actually going to the gym." I dip my head toward the doors.

"Ah. I hope you have a membership badge. They won't let you in without it unless you work there. Lucky for Sabrina there's an override code on the entry boxes. Only a few staff members know the code, mostly managers. She was always forgetting her badge, so one of the managers gave her the code. I think he was tired of having to let her in." Mac laughs. "She even left the badge here on more than one occasion."

"She did?" I ask.

"Yeah, she had a habit of leaving it on the counter here when she got her coffee." He holds up a finger. "In fact…" He dips down out of view. I hear him rustling through things back there, and then he reemerges holding an ID badge. "Here it is."

"You have Sabrina's ID badge for the gym?" That means he could have used it to get inside the gym Thursday night and kill Sabrina. He had means and opportunity. The question is did he have a motive to want her dead?

CHAPTER EIGHT

I know I should give the badge to Quentin or, better yet, call him and have him get the badge directly from Mac so my fingerprints aren't on it, but how do I discreetly do that without people seeing us together? My mind races, trying to come up with a solution.

"Mac, I think you should give that to Detective Perry at the Bennett Falls PD."

"Why's that?"

I can't exactly tell him he's a suspect now. There's no way he'd implicate himself like that. And if I walk away, he could dispose of the badge so there's no evidence linking him to the murder.

I wave a hand in the air. "You're right. I guess there is no reason to. I can return it to the gym for you. I'm assuming they'll want it back."

He hesitates for a moment, and I'm not sure he believes me, so I add, "Could I get another Americano as well? I could use a little caffeine to jumpstart my brain this morning. I feel like I'm still half asleep." I force out a yawn to sell the story.

Mac bobs his head and finally places the ID badge on the counter. As soon as his back is turned to make my drink, I grab the badge and pocket it. Yes, my fingerprints are now on it, but I don't think Quentin will let anyone accuse me of anything. So help him if he does!

"Here you go," Mac says.

I hand him a five-dollar bill. "Keep the change," I say.

"That's very kind of you."

"Hey, I'm happy to help out a fellow coffee lover." I smile and start in the direction of the gym. I can feel Mac's eyes on me as I walk away. I use Samantha's badge to get in the front door of the gym. It's a proxy card, so you don't have to swipe it. It reads the card from a few feet away. As soon as I hear the click of the lock release, I grab the door and open it, disappearing from Mac's view. I pocket the badge immediately as well because I don't want anyone to have the opportunity to even get a glimpse of Samantha's picture.

Trying to act like I belong, I smile at the girl positioned at the front desk. Of course, I'm not wearing workout clothes, and I don't have a gym bag of any kind that could be holding a change of clothes. She furrows her brow at me.

I gently palm-slap my forehead. "I'm so glad the gym reopened. I left my bag in a locker here a few days ago.

I'm such a scatterbrain." It's like using Samantha's ID is making me channel her inner ditz.

"I hate to break it to you, but the women's locker room is still closed. The police allowed us to reopen the rest of the gym, but the locker room is off-limits until further notice."

"Oh, yeah, I heard someone died here Thursday night. That's just awful. I hope it wasn't because they overdid their workout." Yeah, I sound like a complete idiot. I even grab a strand of hair and twirl it around my finger. The entire performance is making me want to vomit.

"I'm not allowed to talk about it with members. Sorry."

"I get it. No problem."

"If you leave me your name and number, I'll call you when the locker room reopens, and you can get your stuff," she offers.

"Oh, that's okay. I think I'll just go see if my workout partner is here. I should let her know I'm not exactly equipped to join her this morning."

"If you tell me her name, I can let you know if she's here. The badges are linked to your names, so when you scan one, it lets us know you're here."

"Really? I didn't know that." That means the gym would know if Sabrina's badge was used on Thursday night. Quentin needs to know about this, if he doesn't already.

"Well, no need to check on my friend. She texted me

to say she was on her way, and that was"—I pretend to check my phone—"over twenty minutes ago. Wow, I guess I lost track of time when I stopped for coffee." I hold up the to-go cup as evidence.

"You know, it's weird you still have your ID badge if you left your bag here," the girl says, cocking her head at me. "And I don't really remember seeing you here before."

"I typically come in the evenings," I say, hoping the fact that she's here in the morning means she usually works this shift. "My hours at work changed, and I had to adjust my workout time accordingly. Hence the coffee." I force a laugh. "I'm not a morning person."

"And your workout partner was able to change her routine as well? How's that for luck?"

"Oh, she's a stay-at-home mom, and her mother lives next door, so she has a babysitter just about whenever she needs one." I'm not sure how I'm coming up with all of this on the spot, but the lies are pouring out of me at this point. I used to be really bad at acting. I'm not sure if it's a good thing that I've gotten pretty good at it.

"I guess she's the lucky one then," the girl says.

"Yeah, well, I shouldn't take up any more of your time. I don't want you to get in trouble for talking to me instead of working." I start for the glass door leading into the free weight room.

"Talking to members is my job, so it's no worry," she calls after me.

I keep walking, my head down, pretending I'm

reading something on my phone. I don't want to make eye contact with anyone in case they're as chatty as the girl at the front desk. There are only a few people using the free weights, and a quick scan shows the fifteen-pound weight is missing from the set. I walk over to the rack.

"Great, I don't see the fifteen-pound weight," I say loudly enough for the male employee who is spotting a guy at the weight bench to hear.

He tells the guy to wait and walks over to me. "Did you say you're looking for the fifteen-pound weight?" he asks me.

"Yeah."

He stares at me in confusion. "You don't look like you could handle working out with that weight. Are you sure that's the one you use?"

"Oh, um, no. It's not for me. My lifting buddy uses it. I use the five-pound weight."

He bobs his head. "Okay, I just wanted to make sure. I don't want anyone getting injured on my watch."

"Thanks. I appreciate that. Sabrina usually helps me out. I'm sort of new to this."

"Oh, was Sabrina your trainer?"

"Not officially. I met her after one of the classes she taught. She corrected my form on a few exercises. We sort of hit it off, and she'd come talk to me for a while each evening while I got my workout in."

"I'm surprised your workout partner didn't help you. If he or she was using fifteen-pound weights, I'd assume they'd know what they're doing." He crosses his arms, his biceps practically bulging out of the short sleeve gym shirt.

Again, I have to scramble to get out of this mess I've put myself in. "Actually, Sabrina was the one I was talking about."

He narrows his eyes. "You lifted with Sabrina?"

"Yeah. She told me she'd be here this morning."

"When did you talk to her last?" he asks.

"Um, Thursday, I think it was. I couldn't come here on Friday. I had to work all day. And Saturdays are my day off."

"Then I hate to be the one to break this to you, but Sabrina died Thursday night."

I bring my hand to my mouth. "Oh no. How?"

"That's why the gym was closed Friday and Saturday. I guess you didn't hear."

"No, I didn't. Work has been crazy. I can't believe this. What happened?"

The guy's name tag says Chris. I'll have to try to get a list of employees from the gym's website. I'm not sure I'll find one, though.

"I'm not allowed to say. Sorry."

I reach for his arm. "But she was my friend. Can't you tell me anything?"

He looks around, his eyes going to a camera in the corner. He picks up the five-pound weight and rambles on about some curling exercise. At first, I'm not sure what he's doing, but then I realize he's making sure it looks like he's assisting me with a workout in case anyone reviews the camera footage.

He hands me the weight. "You try it."

"I'm not exactly dressed to work out. My gym bag is in the women's locker room, and I was told I couldn't get in there today."

"That's correct. It's still blocked off by the police."

"I'm just having the worst day. I can't believe Sabrina is gone."

"I guess you knew her pretty well."

"Yeah. Would you excuse me? I need to use the restroom."

"You'll have to use the family restroom in the middle of the locker room entrances," he says.

I nod and walk toward the hallway off the weight room. There's police tape across the door to the women's locker room. I place my to-go cup in the garbage can and discreetly look around for cameras or anyone who might be watching. I don't see either, so I quickly dash into the women's locker room.

Every single locker door is open. A few have personal belongings inside. I'm assuming the police looked through everything for evidence already. In the back of the locker room, after the bathroom stalls and sinks, is the entrance to the showers. There are still markers on the floor, indicating where Sabrina's body was discovered. I walk over to them. Crime scenes aren't really my thing. I'm not sure what to look for. The police have already combed over every inch of the space, so I doubt I'll find anything they didn't.

It looks like Sabrina was intending to shower when she was attacked. Quentin's confirmed the murder weapon was the fifteen-pound weight they discovered Sabrina's blood on. What else could there be to get from this scene? I look up, noticing there's an exit on the opposite side of the showers. Members can actually leave through a small hallway out of the locker rooms. I walk over to it. You need an ID badge to get out. I guess that's another way they keep tabs on who's here and who leaves. I know better than to swipe Samantha's badge to see what this exit looks like. If anyone catches me with this thing, I could wind up in serious trouble. Especially since I have Sabrina's badge on me as well.

I walk through the shower stalls, just so I can say I looked at the entire crime scene. Then I head back to the lockers. The only mirrors in this place are at the sinks, so it's not like Sabrina would have seen someone sneaking up on her in the reflection of any mirrors. Plus, if she was the last one to leave for the night, she probably assumed she was alone in the locker room.

I don't know why I even risked coming in here. My time is better spent talking to Sabrina's coworkers. I'm not sure if any of her clients would be here on a Sunday morning, but I could discreetly ask around about that as well. I wish I'd thought to change into workout clothes before I came, though. I must look very suspicious walking around a gym in jeans. At least I'm not wearing a Cup of Jo shirt today. That's a plus.

Unsure what else to look at in the locker room, I walk toward the exit leading back to the hallway. Leaving is going to be much harder than getting into the locker room since I can't make sure the coast is clear before opening the door. And considering the door has police tape across it, I can't even pretend I didn't know I was going in the wrong door and claim to be new to the gym.

I take a deep breath and slowly open the door a crack, but it goes swinging wide open, making me jump back.

"What were you doing in there?" the girl from the front desk asks me.

"Oh, I um—"

"I told you the women's locker room was closed, not to mention there's police tape across the doors. Get out of there now."

I step out into the hallway. A woman stares at us as she walks toward the exit.

"I just thought I could grab my bag really quickly," I try to explain.

The girl looks at my empty hands. "I don't know why you'd think that would be okay since this is a crime scene, but you don't even have your bag with you now."

"I know. It wasn't there." I jerk my thumb over my shoulder. "I guess I was wrong about leaving it here. It must be in the back of my friend's car."

"Where is your workout partner?" she asks, and it's

obvious she's now questioning every single part of the story I told her when I arrived.

"I think she's in the bathroom." It's a stupid thing to say since we're standing right next to said bathroom, and this girl could easily check.

She narrows her eyes at me, clearly not believing a word I'm saying. "What's your name?"

"Samantha Shaw," I say, hoping Samantha has never actually stepped foot in here since getting her membership.

The girl holds out her hand. "Let me see your ID badge."

Oh, this is not helping my situation. "Okay, but I dyed my hair since I joined the gym, so I look a little different." I reach into my back pocket and pull out the badge. I swallow hard as I hand the ID to the woman. "I used to wear colored contacts, too. I don't anymore." Could Samantha and I look any more different? This is never going to work.

The girl peers at the photo on the badge. "How did you get this? This ID badge belongs to Sabrina Kincade, and I know for a fact she didn't have it on her Thursday evening because I saw her use the keycode to get in."

I'm not sure how I'm going to explain this one.

The woman holds up her hand and grabs her cell phone from her back pocket. "Don't move. I'm calling the police."

This just went from extremely bad to absolute worst-case scenario in a matter of seconds.

CHAPTER NINE

The girl brings me to the front desk while we wait for the police to arrive. Her boss, a man named Winston Alpine according to his name tag, bombards me with questions.

"Where did you get Sabrina's ID badge?"

"She misplaced it. I was holding on to it to return to her," I say, not wanting to give him any details.

"You should have turned it in to the front desk."

"Shouldn't it go to the police?" I ask. "They certainly won't be happy to know so many people have handled it now." I shouldn't be giving him a hard time when he could press charges against me for impersonating a member and trespassing at the gym, but I hate when people treat me like a criminal.

"That's not your concern at this time," he says through gritted teeth.

"Where is your ID badge? Or do you not actually belong to this gym?"

"I'd prefer to speak with the police if you don't mind." I cross my arms and turn my head away from him.

"I actually do mind because this is my place of business."

I face him head-on. "Yes, where one of your employees was murdered Thursday night."

"I'm well aware."

"And what have you done to help solve the murder?" I ask. "I know your cameras were disabled thanks to the power outage, but surely there's something you can do to aid in the investigation."

"That isn't your concern, now is it?"

"Is it *your* concern?" I ask. "Because it certainly doesn't seem like it. Is it possible there was bad blood between you and Sabrina? Are you afraid of what the police will find out if you offer any information—"

He holds up a hand. "You can stop right there. You were caught—on camera might I add—entering a crime scene that was clearly marked off in addition to one of my employees telling you it was off-limits. You have no right to come into my gym, which you clearly aren't a member of, and accuse me of anything. Am I making myself clear?"

"I suppose if I ask any of your employees, not a single one of them will be able to tell me about any problems between you and Sabrina."

He leans down so he's right in my face. "Who do you

think you are? You're not a police officer. You have no business sticking your nose into this."

"Into what exactly?" I ask, showing him I'm not intimidated in the least by him.

Before he can answer, someone taps on the gym door.

"The police are here," the girl at the front desk says before using a button on the security pad in front of her to let Quentin in.

"Don't move," Winston says, wagging his finger at me before turning to face Quentin.

Quentin holds up his badge. "Detective Perry." His gaze falls on me, and I swear his jaw clenches so hard he might have chipped a tooth or two. "Is this the woman you found snooping around?"

"Not just snooping around. She had the badge of the woman who died here Thursday night," Winston says.

"I'll need that badge." Quentin removes a plastic bag from his pocket and opens it so Winston can drop the badge inside it. Then Quentin zips the bag and returns it to his pocket. "I'll take her from here." He waves a hand at me.

"That's it?" Winston asks. "She had a dead woman's badge and used it to get into my gym."

"No, she didn't," the girl at the desk says. "According to our security system, Sabrina's badge hasn't been used today."

Winston looks at me. "How did you get in then?"

"I have a membership. I wasn't trespassing at all." I

walk over to Quentin. "I'll be happy to show the detective here."

Since Quentin knows exactly what badge I used, and he definitely doesn't want to bring Samantha into any of this or get himself in hot water, he opens the door for me.

"Hold on. I want her membership revoked. This isn't over." Winston's face is bright red.

"I assure you the BFPD will take care of this matter. Once we're finished, you can revoke the woman's membership, but I think you can agree that an open murder investigation takes precedence at the moment." His tone makes it clear he isn't willing to negotiate on this.

Winston clears his throat. "Very well."

Quentin leads me to his patrol car.

"I'm not getting in the back of that car," I say.

"Actually, you are because they called the police on you. If I don't bring you to the station and question you, I'm going to have Chief Harvey breathing down my neck, asking me a bunch of questions neither one of us can answer."

As much as I hate it, he's right. He opens the back door of the patrol car for me, and I get inside with a huff. He slams the door, and I whip out my phone to call Cam.

"Hey? How did it go?"

"Well, I'm in the back of Quentin's patrol car on my way to the station for questioning, so about as badly as it could go."

"I'm on my way," Cam says. "I swear I'll kill Quentin for this."

"While I appreciate the offer, it's not his fault this time."

Quentin eyes me in the rearview mirror and shakes his head as he drives.

"I may have gotten myself into some trouble."

"I'll be there soon," Cam says.

I end the call and lean my head back on the seat.

"What were you thinking, Jo?" Quentin asks.

"You sent me there!"

"Don't start. I don't know how I'm going to get you out of this mess right now. I need to think." He doesn't say a word for the rest of the drive to the station.

I catch a glimpse of the new chief of police as Quentin brings me into an interrogation room. He has salt and pepper hair and a beard to match. He's pretty average in height. I'd guess around five foot eleven. The most intimidating thing about him is that his face looks like it's carved in stone, as if a single smile might crack his skin completely. If I had to guess, I'd say he's trying to appear tougher than he is to prove himself in his new position.

"Sit," Quentin tells me as he shuts the door behind us.

"I'm not a criminal." Still, I sit anyway.

"How did you get yourself into this mess?" he asks, pacing the small space between the table and the two-way mirror.

I ignore his question and jump into the details he needs to know. "The gym has everyone's badge linked to their membership ID number or name. Something like that. They know who used a badge to get in Thursday evening. You need to get their records and find out who came to the gym that night. I know for a fact that Sabrina didn't have her ID badge on her. She used the keycode pin to get in instead."

"Because *you* were found with Sabrina's badge," Quentin says. "Do you realize how that looks?"

"I got it from Mac."

Quentin stops pacing and stares at me. "Who?"

"The coffee truck guy. Gerald MacLean. Ask him about it. He said Sabrina left the ID badge in the window of his truck Thursday evening. He's had it ever since. He could have used it to get inside the gym and kill her."

"The coffee truck guy?" Quentin asks. "Seriously, Jo? What are you doing, trying to frame your competition now?"

"Don't be absurd, Quentin."

"Then tell me what evidence you have to prove this guy did anything to Sabrina Kincade."

"I just did! The badge. His fingerprints will be on it."

"And so will yours," he counters. "Still want me to run the badge for prints? Chief Harvey will have you put on the list of suspects."

"This is crazy." I lean forward and whisper, "I'm helping you. You can't let that happen."

"You're lucky I don't have this conversation being recorded," he says.

"I think you mean *you're* lucky. I'm not the one who could lose my job over this."

"No, you're the one who could wind up in jail because of this."

Touché. "What do we do then? Have you checked to see if anyone used the exit in the locker room Thursday night? I'm assuming the killer left that way because it's the quickest escape route.

"The power went out. It's most likely that the killer didn't need to use a badge to exit the building."

Just wonderful. "Mac's truck is parked right outside the gym. He would have been able to use Sabrina's badge to get into the gym before the power went out. Then he could have left through the locker room exit without anyone seeing him."

"I'll check with the front desk girl and see when Sabrina's keycard was last used," he says, jotting down a note in his pad.

"Find out which clients she saw that night as well."

"That I already know."

"And you didn't think to send me that list of names so I could talk to those people?"

"Sure, let me do that now since you going to the gym worked out so well for us both." He runs a hand through his hair.

"I know it went as badly as it could have. I don't know what you want me to say except I'm sorry."

He sighs. "You know they can use their security system to find out it was Samantha's badge that got you inside the gym."

"Have her call the gym and say she lost her ID badge."

He nods. "Good thinking." He whips out his phone, and I assume he's texting her to do just that.

"By the way, how did you manage to get her to drop off those flowers without saying the real purpose for them? It was so not like her."

"I told her I'd explain after she delivered them and went back to her shop."

Ah, that makes sense. It also explains why she was sniffling when she delivered the flowers. She was upset. "She didn't think you were really giving me flowers, did she?"

"At first, but when I told her what really happened, she was kind of excited to be part of the secret."

Now we have to hope that excitement doesn't lead to her telling people about her part in it. I don't mention that to Quentin, though, because he's clearly stressed out enough as it is.

"How do I get myself out of this situation?" I ask.

"For starters, you never step foot inside that gym again," Quentin says.

"Well, that's obvious. What about the supposed theft of badges, though?"

"I'll write up a report that you found both badges after their owners misplaced them. Sam uses the mechanic on Lake View so you can say you found the badge on the sidewalk."

"I might have given Sam's name to the front desk girl," I say, and Quentin cringes.

He presses his lips together, most likely to keep from screaming at me.

"It was when she caught me coming out of the locker room, so maybe I could say I was scared and not thinking straight. You know, like the name on the badge I found that morning was fresh on my mind so I said that instead of my own."

"Basically, make you seem like you're a complete airhead who was afraid of being caught and thrown in jail. I can do that."

He has plenty of experience explaining his wife's airhead behavior, so this should be a piece of cake for him.

"Great. Can I go then?"

"You trespassed on a crime scene, Jo. If I don't address that, the chief will haul me into his office before you step foot outside this station."

"I've helped the BFPD before. Can't you let me off with a warning this time?"

He huffs. "I might be able to get away with a strongly worded written reprimand and a fine."

"A fine?" This is crazy. "Quentin, you sent me in there. With Samantha's ID badge I might add. I'm in this situation because of you."

"I know. I'll pay the fine. I have to put the paperwork through, though."

I shake my head. "Do what you have to do." I cross my arms and lean back in the seat.

"Give me a few minutes. I'll be back." He walks out, leaving me alone.

Everyone tells me, practically on a daily basis, to kick Quentin and Samantha out of my life for good. Why don't I listen to them? I don't owe either of them anything after the way they betrayed me, and yet here I am sticking my neck out on the line for Quentin.

The door opens, and Cam walks in. "Hey." He rushes over and pulls me into a hug. "Are you okay?"

"I can't believe Quentin let you in here," I say.

"I didn't give him a choice. I said he could let me in, or I could make a huge scene in the middle of the station. He's clearly afraid of the new chief because he took me right here."

"He's writing up a report and slapping me with a fine."

"But you were only at the gym because you were helping him!"

"I know. He's going to pay the fine. It's all for show for the new chief."

"I can't believe this."

"I can't either."

Forty minutes later, we're back at Cup of Jo. Some-how, Mickey heard I was brought to the station in the back of Quentin's patrol car, so my coffee shop is packed with people waiting to hear my side of the story.

"Alright, guys," Cam says. "Jo's been through an ordeal. Let's give her some space."

"Jo, you say the word, and we'll storm the station." Mickey is fired up.

"Mickey, I'm fine. I found a few ID badges for gym members, and I might have used one to get into the gym and check out the crime scene."

Mrs. Marlow laughs. "I bet you found more than the police did, too. They should be thanking you."

"Yeah, well that's not going to happen because the new chief doesn't want any consultants helping with cases."

"Is that why Quentin banned you from the case?" Mickey asks.

I nod. "He tried to help me out at the station so I didn't get in trouble."

They all seem to ponder that for a moment.

"What are you going to do, Jo?" Robin asks.

I thought about this long and hard on the drive back after I picked up my car at the gym. "I'm going to do what I should have done a long time ago. I'm going to hang up my detective's cap."

CHAPTER TEN

The collective gasp that rings through Cup of Jo is almost deafening.

"You can't be serious," Jamar says. "Without you, murderers would be running free in this town."

"He's right, Jo," Mrs. Marlow says. "You can't leave us in the hands of Quentin Perry. We might as well pack up and move."

Mo and Wes come rushing into Cup of Jo. The second she spots me, Mo runs over and throws her arms around me. "I'm going to kill him. For real this time. I have had it with that man."

"Calm down, Mo. I'm fine. Quentin took care of it."

"He's done plenty, and it has to end."

"I agree, which is why I'm taking myself off this case and all future cases."

Mo's eyes widen. "Who do you think you're kidding?"

"No one. I'm serious. I'm done with all of it." I walk to the counter and start scrubbing it even though it's already clean.

Mo follows me with Cam and Wes on her heels. "Jo Coffee doesn't walk away from anything without a fight."

"I did fight, and I lost. I'm tired of losing things because of Quentin."

The door opens, and Quentin walks in. Speak of the devil. The mob of people immediately surround him.

"Whoa. Back off. All of you!" he yells.

"Guys!" With one word from me, they all take two steps back. "I appreciate your support, but I've got this. Sit down. Have some coffee."

They listen, but every eye remains trained on Quentin as he approaches me.

He hands me a slip with the fine on it. "I have to personally serve you with this."

I take it and then immediately give it right back. "There. You did. We're done."

He pockets it. "I'll pay it as soon as I leave here, and everything will be fine. You can't be caught anywhere near the case again or the chief will have you arrested, but—"

"That won't be an issue because I'm not working the case anymore."

"What?" He's supposed to pretend to not want my help, but his surprise totally blows that cover.

"I mean it. I'm done. For good. You're going to have to solve this without me."

"Jo…"

I raise my head. "Robin, could you cover the register, please? I'm not feeling well. I'm going home for the day."

"Of course," she says.

Cam wraps his arm around me. "I'll go with you."

Quentin is still staring at me as we walk out.

I don't hear from Quentin all of Sunday night, which hopefully means he got the message. It feels weird going into work knowing I'm going to spend the entire day there. No sneaking off to investigate. No questioning people to find out who would want Sabrina Kincade dead.

I had a dream about her. I also dreamed Mac was driving a giant coffee cup down Main Street, though, so clearly my mind is troubled. I breathe in the scent of baked deliciousness as I step inside Cup of Jo. Cam stayed at my apartment until midnight, and for the first time in a long time, we had a nice evening with no talk of murder. I could get used to that.

Stepping into the kitchen, I notice Cam is looking sluggish. He's not used to staying up late since he's always awake between three and four in the morning. Now I feel bad that I kept him up until midnight. I didn't even consider how it would affect him today. Does that make me a bad girlfriend?

"Hey. You look tired. Are you okay?" I ask him.

He slumps onto the stool by the island. "I'll be fine. Don't worry about it. I wouldn't change getting to spend hours with you without worrying about a case for anything."

I walk over and kiss him. "I'll make you some strong coffee."

"Extra large, please," he says, only one side of his mouth curving up when he attempts to smile.

I cup the side of his face. "You poor baby. Maybe you should go home and take a nap when you're finished stocking the display case."

"I feel old. I remember when I used to pull all-nighters in college. I'm only thirty, but my body can't handle the lack of sleep anymore."

"I know what you mean. I'll get started on that coffee." I hurry back out to set up the coffee machines for the day.

Even though Cup of Jo doesn't open for another thirty minutes, Samantha walks through the door.

"Sorry, but we're still closed," I say, not in the mood to deal with her so early in the morning. I haven't had a sip of caffeine yet.

"But, Jo, you have to help, and Quentin said I can't talk to you about this when people are around."

Did he actually send his pregnant wife here to plead his case for him? The nerve of that man!

"I'm not working on this case with him. End of story. There's nothing to discuss."

"But he got in trouble for going easy on you. Chief

Harvey said you should have had harsher punishment for trespassing at that gym."

The coffee pot finishes brewing enough to pour Cam's cup, so I do, and then I set it in the window for him. "Cam, order up!" I tell him.

"You're a lifesaver. Thank you!" he says, grabbing the coffee and immediately sipping it.

"You might want to put some ice in that if you plan to down it quickly," I say.

He points at me. "Good idea." He hurries off to the big walk-in cooler.

"Jo," Samantha whines.

I whirl around to face her. "I thought you'd left." More like I hoped.

"I can't. Not until you promise to help Quentin. He needs to solve this case."

"I'm not stopping him. In fact, I wish him luck." I want him to solve the case so he'll leave me alone. Maybe for good.

Samantha cradles her baby bump. "But he's moody."

"How is that any different than normal?" I ask.

"He's never moody with me."

That's right. He saves the best of himself for Samantha, and the rest of the human population gets what's left over.

"How can you be so heartless? He got you flowers. Or did you forget?" She tries to cross her arms, but her belly gets in the way. She huffs and lowers her hands to her sides.

"The flowers were to cover up the fact that he was slipping me your gym membership badge so I could do his dirty work. I don't feel bad that he's paying the fine he felt the need to issue me after I got caught. I wouldn't have been there if not for him."

"He did what?" she asks. "Money's been tight with all the baby stuff we need. How much was the fine?"

Great. She's having a rare moment of clarity. I didn't think she worried about money issues or any real adult issues for that matter. She's like a big child most of the time.

"I don't know." I really didn't even look at the paper when Quentin handed it to me—or "served it to me" as he said.

"The chief said Quentin"—she looks up and scrunches her forehead—"unnecessarily uses too many outside resources."

Wow. She just recalled a direct quote, too. "Are you on some super strength prenatal vitamins or something?" I ask. Most pregnant women I've known claimed to get scatterbrained, not have heightened memories. But then again, Samantha never was the definition of normal.

"The doctor gave me vitamins. I have to take them every morning. They're huge, and I hate them. They get stuck in my throat." She grimaces and rubs her throat as if one is lodged there right now.

I turn and brew some apricot herbal tea for her. "Here." I hand the cup to her. "It's hot, so be careful."

"Thanks." She brings the cup to the nearest table and

sits down. "Quentin told me he thinks you would have made a better detective than he is. I think he turned down the position as chief of police because of you."

She can't possibly blame me for that. Quentin hated being interim chief. "He told me he felt useless sitting at a desk instead of being out there making a real difference in the world."

"He told me he's not sure he can solve cases without your help anymore. He didn't think he deserved the promotion."

I can't believe he'd say that, but I *really* can't believe he'd admit it to Samantha. He thinks the world of her, and I don't think he'd jeopardize having her think less of him. "Did this all come out in couples' therapy?" I ask her.

She bobs her head. "We're not supposed to talk about this stuff outside of the therapist's office. That's a safe space, but you've always been my best friend, Jo."

"Samantha—"

She holds up both hands. "I know. I remember what you said. We aren't friends anymore. But you're still Jo. You help people. It's what you do. And you're good at figuring things out. You're the closest to perfect someone can get. That's why everyone in this town loves you so much."

I had no idea she saw me that way. I sit down at the table with her. "I'm far from perfect. I have plenty of flaws. And Quentin doesn't need me to solve this case. He's just feeling insecure right now."

"How does he get past that?" she asks.

"Solving this case would be a good start," I say.

She reaches for my hand on the table. "What if he can't? What will happen to him then?" She squeezes so tightly it hurts.

"Easy there," I say, pulling free from her grip. "I have to be able to serve coffee all day."

"I have an idea."

I almost fall out of my chair at that. Samantha isn't the type to come up with plans. "What kind of idea?"

"I overheard Mickey say you were investigating the case behind Quentin's back. Quentin told me that's what you two agreed you'd tell people so it didn't get back to the chief that you were helping Quentin."

I was, but that was before.

"What if you really did go behind Quentin's back, and you solve the case?"

"How would that help his confidence?" If anything, I'd think it would make it worse.

Samantha leans toward me and whispers, "You solve the case but then plant clues so Quentin thinks he solved it."

Part of me wants to stand up and demand to know who this woman is impersonating Samantha Perry, but the fact that she whispered her secret plan to me when we're the only two people around is proof she's still the same Samantha. I really want to know what brand of vitamin her doctor has her on, though, because it's clearly a miracle drug. I've never seen her this able to focus.

"Why aren't you saying anything?" she asks. "Do you not understand the plan?"

I laugh because this feels like such a role reversal it's funny. "I understand it just fine, but I don't think I want to get involved."

She slumps back in her chair. "If you don't, Quentin might lose his job."

"It's not my responsibility to fix this for him." I don't owe Quentin anything. Yet he and Samantha are always making demands of me.

"I know that," she says, surprising me. "But I'm asking you to do this. We used to be close. I could always count on you when I had a problem. Well, I have a problem now, and I don't know who else to turn to. You're my only hope." She rubs her belly. "You're *our* only hope."

She's playing dirty. I'm not sure I like this new version of Samantha because I'm actually considering this plan of hers.

"Okay, look, if I agree to this, then I'm done once Quentin makes an arrest."

"But what if—?"

"There's always going to be another case. Chief Harvey is clearly not going to pay me to consult on cases, so why would I keep spending all my time trying to solve them? Quentin needs a push. He'll be fine after that." He was better at his job before Samantha got pregnant. My guess is he's stressed and sleep-deprived, and that's taking its toll on his work. "I think everything will work itself out soon."

She sighs and thinks for a moment before responding. "I guess you could be right. Does this mean you're going to follow through with my plan?"

I mull it over, trying to come up with another solution, but I fall short. "Yeah. I'll solve the case and plant enough clues for Quentin to think he's solved it himself."

Samantha gets off her stool and hugs me. "Thank you, Jo. I knew I could still count on you. You really are the best." She's still smiling as she walks out of Cup of Jo.

Cam comes out of the kitchen. "I hate to admit to eavesdropping, but did I hear you agree to solve this case and give Quentin the credit?"

"You did. Looks like I'm not hanging up my detective's hat after all."

CHAPTER ELEVEN

I ask Mo and Wes to meet Cam and me at Cup of Jo on their lunch break. Mo, of course, made me fill her in on what's going on, so she already knows I'm back on the case. She's looking into Sabrina Kincade's clients at the gym for me. The problem is finding out who they were. So far, I know where Logan Ross on the custodial crew lives, but I don't think he'd have any clue who Sabrina's clients were since he never actually met her. And it's not like Sabrina was close to her roommate, Jade Summers. They basically were only living together to cut the expense of having a home.

"How is it possible that no one actually knew this woman?" I ask as I finish making an espresso.

"Knew what woman?" Jamar asks me, looking around at Cup of Jo to see whom I'm talking about.

"Sabrina Kincade."

"Woo-hoo!" Mickey says. "Jo's back on the case!"

I turn around to see everyone is staring expectantly at me. I hold up a hand. "Quiet. Quentin has no idea, and he can't know either. No one breathes a word of this outside of these walls. Do you all understand?"

"Stick it to him, Jo," Mrs. Marlow says. For a seventy-year-old woman, she certainly is feisty.

"That's sort of the opposite of my plan. I'm going to let Quentin take credit for this case, but I'll be feeding him information without him realizing it."

"How do you plan to do that?" Mrs. Marlow asks.

"Forget *how*," Mickey says. "*Why* would you do that?"

"Okay, look, guys, I know none of you is a fan of Detective Perry, and I'll spare you the details, but he needs this win. You don't have to get involved, but you do have to keep your mouths shut about what I'm doing. It's that simple."

"We trust you, Jo." Mrs. Marlow pats my hand on the counter and takes the espresso from me.

"Thank you. Now if anyone gets wind of anything related to Sabrina Kincade's murder, I'd like to know about it."

"And how do you plan to get information to Quentin?" Mickey asks.

I cock my head at him. "I'm pretty sure you theorizing about things in his presence might help."

He bobs his head. "Consider it done."

"And there's always Samantha as well." The entire coffee shop goes quiet, and all heads turn to me. "Has no one talked to her recently?" I ask. "She's on some superpowered prenatal vitamins that have her thinking more clearly than ever."

"That makes sense now," Mickey says, wagging a finger in the air. "I heard Erica Daniels and a few other teachers at the high school talking about how they ordered flowers from Bouquets of Love, and it was the first time Samantha didn't ask them to repeat the order three times. Erica even confirmed that she'd gotten it right the first time."

I bob my head. "She's onboard with this. It was actually her plan."

"Jo, you've got to tell us why, though," Mrs. Marlow says. "You know we'll support you no matter what, but give us something here."

"It's the new chief of police. He seems to have it out for Quentin."

Mrs. Marlow stands up tall, which isn't tall at all, but I wouldn't mess with her regardless. "A newbie is trying to mess with one of our own?"

"Exactly." This is why I love my little town. We're one big happy family. Mostly.

"Not on my watch. I'll choose you over Quentin every time, sugar, but I'll choose Quentin over this outsider who wants to come in here and change our town."

Heads bob all around the café in agreement.

"Good. I knew I could count on all of you," I say.

A few minutes later, everyone has their coffees and baked goods, and conversations return to usual topics.

Jamar carries a bin of empty coffee mugs to the kitchen, but he pauses by me and whispers, "You're like their queen or something." He laughs and enters the kitchen.

I'm still laughing when Samantha walks up to the counter. "Morning, Jo."

"Morning, Samantha. What can I get for you?"

She looks around the café and then lowers her voice when she says, "Information." It's like watching a really bad spy movie.

"How about tea?" I suggest, turning to make it for her.

She follows me down the line of coffee machines to the pot of hot water for tea. "Apricot, please."

I take out the tea bag, place it into the to-go cup, and pour the hot water. I turn and hand it to her. "On the house."

"Thanks, Jo. I was hoping you could tell me your plan for today."

"It's probably best if I don't."

"I want to help, though."

I don't think there's anything she can do to help. Unless… "Can I borrow your gym badge again?" Quentin took it back when I was brought into the station. He didn't want anyone to know I had it on me because it connected him to my presence at the gym.

"Sure. I'll send it over." She winks at me and walks away.

"That was weird," Robin says, preparing a tea behind me.

"She's very strange lately. Pregnancy is definitely taking its toll on her in some odd ways."

"I think I prefer her the way she was. She wasn't the wittiest, but she was always smiling and nice to people."

Robin's right. I think that's why I liked Samantha when I first met her. Despite people picking on her in school, she was always smiling. And if someone dropped their books in the hallway, Samantha would be the first to rush over and help them pick them up again. Sometimes it's really hard not to be bitter about how Quentin and Samantha's cheating cost me two good friends.

I wait for Samantha's return or for her to deliver the gym badge, but hours pass with no sign of either. Mo and Wes show up at lunchtime, and we take the corner table. Cam joins us, bringing some apple strudel he just took out of the oven. Of course, I make enough coffee to go around.

"Okay, so Sabrina was a pretty quiet person," Mo begins. "She didn't even interact with many people online. Her social media profiles are mostly memes she found funny. She does have some friends listed there, but it's mostly people she went to high school with. Various high schools I should mention. She was tossed around a lot in the foster care system."

"That means none of those people were likely good friends with her," I say.

"My thoughts exactly. There's really no interaction other than a few likes on a post. No comments at all."

"That's sad," Wes says. "I can't imagine not having

any real friends in life. When I first moved here for my new job, I hated not knowing anyone." He bumps his shoulder into Mo's. "I was really grateful when this one offered to show me around and introduce me to some great people."

"Little did you know those people would get you wrapped up in so many murder cases," I say before sipping my coffee.

"You're right. That part I couldn't predict, but I wouldn't change it." He smiles at Mo again.

I swear if she and Wes get engaged before Cam and I do… Maybe she's right, and I should ask Cam. Once this case is behind us. I don't want to pop the question in the middle of a murder investigation. That doesn't exactly scream romantic to me.

"I asked Samantha to let me borrow her gym badge to see if there's anything special about the security system they use over there," I say.

"Good thinking," Mo says. "We can probably analyze the card and figure out what kind of system they're using and how easy it might be to hack."

"The cards feed back to their internal security system, which is linked to their members' information."

Mo's eyes widen. "Then I can probably find out who was always at the gym the same time as Sabrina by pairing up when their IDs were used to access the building."

"You can do that?" I ask.

"Your sister has some mad hacking skills," Wes says.

"How did I not know this about you?" I ask.

Mo shrugs. "I don't like to brag." She can't hold back her smile.

"Yes, you do," I say with a laugh.

Samantha walks into Cup of Jo, carrying a small vase of flowers. "Jo, I have the first sample arrangement for you," she says, bringing it over to me.

Mo's eyes widen in disbelief. I'm right there with her because Sam's ruse about me wanting vases of flowers for Cup of Jo is genius. Of course, it's also unnecessary since I told everyone in here what's really going on.

She places the vase in front of me. "What do you think?" She winks.

"I think it's beautiful. Let's go with this one. I'll take one for the counter, one for the display case, and one for by the door. I could put it on one of those pretty white pedestals I've always wanted to get."

"So that's," she pauses, and I see a glimpse of the old Samantha. Math was never her strong suit.

"Three, but I'll put this one in the kitchen for Cam, so make it three additional vases." That way no one sees me remove the gym badge from this bouquet. I'd rather not let anyone know my sister plans to hack the gym's security system. I trust my customers, but word could still get back to the new chief of police somehow, and I'm not letting Mo get locked up because of this case.

"You got it. Do you want to pay now or later?" she asks.

Oh, so we're really going through with this? "Um,

later, I guess." I suppose the flowers would make the place look nice, so why not?

"I'll get started on the arrangements right away then." She turns on her heel and walks out.

I stand up. "Mo, would you help me bring these into the kitchen?"

She stands up. "Sure?" It comes out as a question, probably because carrying a small vase isn't exactly a two-person job. She leans toward me and whispers, "How exactly am I supposed to be assisting you with this particular task?"

"No clue. Just wing it."

She pretends to adjust a few of the flowers while we walk, and she rambles about the colors and arrangement.

Once we're inside the kitchen, I place the vase on the counter and search for the card. Like the last bouquet Samantha delivered, there's a plastic card holder with an envelope on the end. I pull out the envelope and remove the card from it.

"Here." I hand it to Mo. "And whatever you do, don't get caught. Quentin doesn't have much pull with the new chief, and he's already in trouble for going easy on me. I'm not sure he'd be able to bail you out if the gym finds out you're hacking into their system."

"I'll admit this might put my skills to the test, and I'm going to have to use my work computer to pull it off, which doesn't exactly sit well with me, but I'll do my best."

"Are you sure about this?"

She pockets the card. "Piece of cake."

"You don't have to downplay how difficult it's going to be," I say.

"No, I want a piece of cake. To go. For my troubles," she says. "One for Wes, too." She walks out of the kitchen.

The rest of the day is rather uneventful. There's not much I can do until Mo manages to get the names of Sabrina's clients for me. It would be so much easier if I could ask Quentin for the list of client names, but that would put him in the mix again. I'm not willing to bet Samantha could get the information I need without tipping off Quentin either. She might be Samantha 2.0 right now, but she's still Samantha.

"No word from Mo?" Cam asks me.

"Not a one." I'm about to tell him how useless I feel when Mac walks into Cup of Jo.

Cam and I exchange a look. With the gym back open, he should be manning his coffee truck.

"Mac, what are you doing here?" I ask him.

He rubs his hands together. "Well, I thought I should check out your place." He looks around. "I like the décor. And it appears you're full to capacity."

"Speaking of, why aren't you at your coffee truck?" I ask, placing my hands on the counter.

"I'm thinking Bennett Falls isn't the coffee truck kind of town. Other than Sabrina, I don't have many regular customers." He bobs one shoulder. I even saw quite a few people carrying to-go cups from here into the gym this morning. I thought maybe that was a sign."

"A sign of what exactly?"

"Of two things, really. First, I need to try your coffee. Second, I need a new profession. Or a new town. I'm not sure which just yet."

"We aren't trying to run anyone out of town," Cam assures him.

Mac holds up a hand. "Oh, I know you're not. You seem like good people." He scans the menu board. "Let's see. I think I'll try your Americano since you tried mine," he says.

"Coming right up." I turn to make his drink, finishing it off by adding a chocolate straw to the cup. He pulls his wallet out of his back pocket.

"It's on the house," I say.

"Oh, I couldn't." He removes a few bills.

"I insist."

He takes two singles and places them in my tip mug. "I never thought to put out a tip jar. I guess I still have a lot to learn. This was a thing I decided to do now that I'm no longer in the service." He seems almost lost, and I can't help feeling bad for him. But at the same time, if he was in the service, there's a chance he's had to take lives before. I know I'm biased because he's my competition, but I can't remove him from my suspect list yet.

"Hey, Mac, did you ever notice the same people coming and going from the gym at the time Sabrina was usually there?" I ask.

"I can't say I really paid much attention. I admit I watch a lot of true crime shows on my phone while I'm sitting in my truck. I love those shows."

Okay, yes, I watch them, too, but I like solving crimes. What if he watches them for a completely different reason? He might be trying to get pointers for how to pull off the perfect murder.

"What got you interested in crime shows?" I ask, and Cam discreetly reaches for my hand.

"Oh, I don't know. Something about unsolved crimes fascinates me. I mean in this digital age, you'd think crimes would be easy to solve. But take Sabrina's death for instance. The power was out on Thursday night, and because of that, anyone could have snuck into the gym and killed her without there being any evidence on the security feeds. Something as simple as a power outage could make this crime unsolvable." He sips his Americano.

"I don't plan to let that happen," I say with enough venom in my tone that Cam squeezes my hand.

Mac's eyes widen, and I think he's going to have a witty response about my threat, but instead he says, "I'm conceding defeat. You are the reigning coffee queen." He places his free hand on his midsection and bows to me, careful not to spill his drink. "I'm packing up my truck and finding a new town. It was good to meet you both. I wish you a lot of luck with this place, but it doesn't seem like you need any." He turns and walks out.

My prime suspect is fleeing town.

CHAPTER TWELVE

I'm not sure if Quentin could force Mac to stay in town on suspicion alone, but considering I can't even tell Quentin what I think about Mac's involvement in Sabrina's murder, it doesn't matter.

I walk into the kitchen, where I grab my phone and call Samantha. Cam follows me.

"Hey, Jo," she answers. "I can't remember the last time you called me."

Years ago, before she ruined our friendship. "I need you to call Quentin and tell him to get you a tea from the coffee truck by Fantasy Fitness."

"Why? Can't you make me one?" she asks.

"I can, but the owner of the coffee truck is leaving town, and I think he might have been the one who murdered Sabrina Kincade."

She gasps. "If he's leaving town, how can Quentin get me tea from the man's coffee truck?"

"He won't be able to, but it will let Quentin know Mac left. If he really is running to avoid being questioned by the police, Quentin will see his sudden departure as suspicious and hopefully follow up with it."

"Oh. I think I understand. Okay, I'll call him now."

"Thank you, and please call me back to let me know what he said."

"I will." She ends the call.

"You really think Mac killed Sabrina?" Cam asks.

"You heard what he said about the power outage. It's a little too coincidental that he likes unsolved crimes and made the connection that the loss of power would kill the security surveillance the night Sabrina died."

"I have to agree that is a little coincidental," Cam says.

"Exactly. And why pick up and leave now if he's not guilty?"

"Maybe his coffee truck really is hurting for business, and he decided to pack it in." The timer on the oven goes off, and Cam hurries over to take out a tray of crumb cake.

I'm staring at my phone, waiting for Samantha's call. It seems to take forever before it rings. "What did he say?" I answer.

"He kept telling me to go to Cup of Jo, but I insisted the coffee truck guy had better tea. Sorry about that."

"It's fine. Is he going?"

"Yeah, he's on his way now."

"Do you have any idea where he is in this case? Who

he's looking into? Maybe where he was when you called him?"

"He was at the gym. That's how I finally convinced him to go outside and get my tea."

If Quentin is at the gym, Mac and his coffee truck must have still been there when he arrived. Wait! "Mac said his coffee truck won't move. There's a problem with the engine."

"There's a mechanic on the same road. He might have gotten it fixed," Cam says.

"He told us he couldn't afford it."

"I guess we'll know for sure when Quentin calls Sam back," Cam says, placing the baking tray in the sink to wash.

More waiting. Just what I can't stand.

I hang up with Samantha, telling her to call me back the second she hears from Quentin.

I try to keep busy by serving customers and refilling the display cases with Cam's baked goods. I'm going through the motions, though. I wonder if this is what Quentin felt like when he was stuck behind a desk as interim chief of police. It's awful. I'd much rather be out there, interviewing people and chasing down leads.

Finally, my phone rings. I hand over the order I'm filling to Robin and duck into the kitchen. "It's Sam," I tell Cam as I answer the call. "Hello?"

"I did what you told me. As soon as he called, I told him I had to go call you."

I slap my forehead. "Why would you tell him that? Didn't he ask why you had to talk to me?"

"Yes. He did. I told him you ordered flowers. That was good, right?"

Actually, it was. "Yes. Good job, Samantha. So what did Quentin say?"

"The coffee truck is gone."

Then Mac must have had the engine fixed, or he lied about it in the first place. "Did Quentin think that was suspicious?"

"A little. I told him it didn't look good that the owner left town right after a murder happened so close to his truck."

"What did Quentin say to that?" I ask.

"He said you mentioned something about the coffee truck guy earlier."

"Did he seem like he was going to follow up with that lead?" I ask.

"I think so."

"Good. Thanks, Sam. You did great."

"You called me Sam," she says. "I miss that."

I clear my throat. "I've got to go," I say and end the call.

"You okay?" Cam asks me.

"I'm fine." I pocket my phone. "Quentin is looking into Mac. The plan worked."

"Good. Now we just need to get those names from Mo."

I'm putting dinner on the table when Mo and Wes show up at my apartment.

"It smells great in here," Wes says, handing me the bottle of wine he brought.

"Thanks. I hope you like black bean burritos."

"I love them, but I would have brought margarita mix had I known you were making Mexican food.

Jamar brings a pitcher of margaritas to the table. "Already covered."

"We can save the wine for another time," I tell Wes.

"So, I hate to discuss murder while we eat, but I do have something for you," Mo says. She pulls a sticky note out of her purse. "These are Sabrina's regular clients. Some people sign up for individual workout sessions, but these two meet with her every Thursday evening."

The only thing written on the paper are two names and addresses. I look at the names. "Camille Abrams and Austin Jones."

"I didn't get a chance to look up either online because it was harder than I thought to tap into the gym's system."

"It's okay. I plan to talk to both of them tomorrow. I'll find out what I need then."

"Well, you might want to talk to Camille tonight," Mo says.

I motion to the burritos I'm currently serving to everyone. "I'm about to eat."

"Then do it quickly because Camille hasn't used her ID badge to get into the gym since last Thursday night."

"But Austin has?" Cam asks.

Mo nods.

"Then it's possible Camille killed Sabrina and skipped town," Jamar says.

"Or the murder freaked her out so much she decided to not return to the gym," Cam says, being the usual voice of reason in our group.

"It's probably best that we find out either way sooner rather than later," I say, shoveling a large bite of burrito into my mouth.

"Don't choke," Cam says.

"Yeah, without you, Quentin may never find the killer," Mo says.

About twenty minutes later, Cam and I leave Mo, Wes, and Jamar to clean up dinner. I'm mad I'm missing dessert, which is Cam's key lime mousse pie. Yes, it's every bit as delicious as it sounds. He even partially freezes it to get a really refreshingly cool consistency to it. I should have taken a piece to go.

Camille lives about ten minutes from my apartment, so we get there in no time at all. I breathe a little easier when I see a car parked in the driveway. That's a good sign Camille hasn't left town and is probably home right now. Cam parks behind her, and we hurry to the door to ring the bell. It takes a while before someone answers.

The curtain in the window next to the front door moves, and I get a glimpse of whom I'm assuming is

Camille. She lets go of the curtain and answers the door. "Can I help you?" she asks us, keeping herself positioned behind the door and only peeking her head out.

"I hope so. Are you Camille Abrams?" I ask her.

"Yes."

"I'm Joanna, and this is Camden. We were hoping to talk to you about Sabrina Kincade."

Camille's jaw tenses. "What about her?"

"You were a client of hers, right?" I ask.

"Yes. Sunday, Tuesday, and Thursday nights. Why?"

"Could we maybe come inside and talk?" Cam asks.

"Are you from the gym?" Her gaze volleys between us. "Am I in trouble for something?"

What an odd thing to say. "What would you be in trouble for?" I ask.

"Nothing. I mean I missed Sunday's class, but with Sabrina gone, I didn't think I should go."

"We're not from the gym," I tell her. "We're trying to find out what happened to Sabrina Thursday night."

"I'm not in trouble?" she asks again.

"No." Not yet at least. She has a very guilty conscience for an innocent person, making me question if she does have a reason to feel that way.

Camille opens the door further and lets us in. I take in her appearance for the first time. "I know what you're thinking," she says. "I don't look like I go to the gym three days a week."

I hold a up a hand in defense. "For the sake of full

125

disclosure, my diet consists mostly of coffee and baked goods. Cam and I own Cup of Jo on Main Street."

"I've heard about your place. I've never been there, but everyone raves about it." She closes the front door and then brings us to the kitchen. It's like a chef's heaven in here. She has two ovens, two refrigerators, a large island in the middle, enough counter space to house just about every cooking tool imaginable, and the largest mixer I've ever seen outside of Cam's kitchen.

"This is…" Cam can barely speak.

"I cater for a living. Right out of my home. I hire one of those services to actually go on site and serve the food. I can't exactly handle working the events myself. That's why I started going to the gym. I want to get down to a healthy weight. My doctor is concerned about the stress on my heart. He wants me to get that stomach surgery, but I told him I want to try to lose the weight on my own first. Fantasy Fitness's motto is if you can dream up the body you want, they can make your fantasy a reality." Camille shrugs. "I need that."

"Then why didn't you go to the gym Sunday evening?" I ask.

"I don't feel safe after what happened to Sabrina. It was scary Thursday night."

"What do you mean?" Cam asks.

Is it possible that Camille knows what happened and is too scared to talk to the police? That would certainly explain her guilty conscience. "Camille, were you there when Sabrina was killed?"

Camille breaks down and cries, falling into the chair at the kitchen table. "I don't know."

Cam and I exchange a look before sitting down at the table with her.

"Maybe you could walk us through that night. Tell us what you remember," I say.

Cam grabs a napkin from the holder in the center of the table and hands it to her.

"Thank you," she says before dabbing her eyes and then blowing her nose. She crumbles the napkin in her hand but doesn't throw it away. "We were in the aerobics room. I was on the stair climber. We heard the thunder and saw the flashes of lightning through the windows. It was a scary storm." She sniffles. "Then the power went out. Sabrina told me not to worry because the backup generators would kick on in a minute. We waited and waited, but they didn't come on."

That's odd. The owner of the gym would know there had been a problem with the backup generator. Surely, he would have told Quentin if that were the case. Unless someone knew where the generator was housed and manually turned it off. That would point to an employee being the guilty party, though. If we have to look into everyone who works at the gym, this case could go on for a very long time because it could be any employee, not just one that was on the work schedule Thursday night.

"What happened then?" Cam asks.

"Sabrina told me to go home. She helped me find my

127

way to the exit. I got in my car and drove home after that."

"Do you remember anything else? Did you hear anything strange?"

"I'm not sure. I don't like the dark. Storms scare me, and I was on edge." She hesitates, and I can tell there's more.

"There's something you're holding back on," I say. "What is it? Maybe we can help you figure it out."

"Well, when we were heading to the front door, we heard this noise. Like a clicking sound. Sabrina said it was probably the generator trying to come on. I just assumed she was right. But what if it was someone else in there with us?"

"Were you two the last ones in the gym?" I ask.

"Yes. Thursday nights are slow nights at the gym anyway, but with the storm, there were even fewer people in attendance than usual," she says. "Once the thunder and lightning started, everyone else left. It was just Sabrina and me. Even the front desk girl went home."

Sabrina must have been a manager or had some seniority at the gym for everyone to trust her on her own like that. Of course, with their security system, the front desk girl is really nothing more than a greeter. No one can get in without an ID badge.

Unless the power goes out. Which it did.

This means the killer could have been there before Camille left. If that's true, then Sabrina died very shortly after that. She most likely went to the locker room to quickly rinse off or grab her things before leaving. Employees probably park around back, which would be more easily accessed through the locker rooms.

Working a case like this where I can't talk to the gym owner and find all this out is nearly impossible. I know if I step foot inside the gym, he'll press charges for trespassing, and Quentin won't be able to get me out of it a second time.

I might have to enlist Samantha's help again after all.

CHAPTER THIRTEEN

Tuesday morning, I pull Robin aside because I need a favor from her. If I'm going to convince Samantha to go to the gym and get some answers for me, then I need someone to cover Bouquets of Love. I can't let it get back to Quentin that the flower shop is closed, or he'll start asking questions, and I know he'll come to me looking for answers.

"Is everything okay?" Robin asks as I bring her into the kitchen to talk in private.

"Yes, but I need a favor."

"Sure, whatever you need."

I smirk. "You say that now, but I haven't told you what it is yet."

"Uh-oh." She leans against the counter for support. "Alright, I'm ready. Tell me what you need."

"I need you to work at Bouquets of Love this morning."

"What?" Her head jerks back like I sucker punched her.

"Samantha is the only one with a gym membership to Fantasy Fitness. She can get inside and ask questions."

"Oh, I see. So you need her to go in there and investigate for you." Robin shakes her head. "Jo, no matter how good those vitamins are that she's on, there's no way she can pull this off on her own."

"That's why she won't be on her own. I'll be on the phone with her. She'll have an ear bud in so I can listen in and also tell her what to say."

"Smart thinking. But why am I working at her store? Can't she put a sign on the door? I doubt she'll be gone long."

"She could, but I don't want anyone else to know Samantha isn't next door in Bouquets of Love."

"I get it, but I don't know a thing about floral arrangements."

"You won't be doing any, so you'll be fine. I promise."

She nods.

Cam's already aware of the plan since he and I came up with it last night after we left Camille Abrams's house. He's going to help Jamar with the customers while I sit in the kitchen on the phone with Samantha. But first, I have to bring Robin next door and get Samantha on board with this.

Cam and Jamar both nod to me, which means Cam told Jamar what's going on as well. Robin and I walk out, pretending to be in the middle of a conversation about some television show so no one asks us where we're going.

There's not a single person inside Bouquets of Love. Sometimes I wonder how Samantha stays in business, but I suppose a lot of her orders come over the phone rather than in person.

"Hey, Jo. Hey, Robin," Samantha says, sitting on the stool by the register. "Pretty soon I'm going to need a stool with a back. This is already starting to hurt."

"Well, I have a way you can get up and moving around," I say. I briefly fill her in on the plan.

"Do you really think I can do this?" Samantha asks me.

"I'll be on the phone with you the entire time. Just keep your volume up so I can hear what people are saying. I'll tell you what to ask and how to respond. The only hard part will be not letting them in on the fact that you have me on the phone."

She bobs her head. "Okay. I'll keep my hair down to cover my earbuds. Luckily, I only wear yoga pants these days since I grew out of everything else I own." She scrunches her face. "Have you seen maternity clothes? They're hideous. I swear I'd design a cute line of clothes for pregnant women if I had any idea how to go about doing that."

"You look fine," I say, and she scowls. "I mean you look nice."

"Tell me what I need to do?" Robin says.

"You can let the phone go to voice mail. If any

customers come in, write down what they want, their name and contact number, and tell them I'll call them to follow up."

"I can definitely do that," Robin says.

"Then I guess I should get going." Samantha gives me one last worried look before heading out.

"Thanks for doing this, Robin. You'll still get your share of the tips, so don't worry about that."

"You overpay me as it is. I'm not worried, Jo." She waves me out of the flower shop. "Now go. Call Samantha so you can walk her through this."

I walk back to Cup of Jo. The usual crowd is there, and a few ask me about Robin, inquiring whether she's not feeling well.

"She's fine. She had to take care of something, but she'll be back soon," I tell them. I hope none of them questions my absence or Cam's presence behind the coffee counter.

Cam gives my hand a squeeze as I walk by him into the kitchen. As soon as I'm seated on the stool at the island, I call Samantha.

"Hey, Jo. I'm parking now."

"Good. Remember to relax. No one will suspect anything. If they see your earbuds, tell them you're listening to music on your phone."

"Smart thinking. You're so good at this stuff."

"I've had a lot of practice."

"I'm walking in now."

"Great, but don't narrate. It will make you look suspicious. Just turn up your phone volume as loud as it goes. I'll do the same on my end. Then I should be able to hear everything."

"Okay."

She really needs to stop talking to me. I hear the beep as she uses her ID badge to get inside the gym.

"Don't talk directly to me unless you're alone." I quickly add, "And you don't have to respond to that either. Your silence will be response enough."

"Good morning," a faint voice says through the phone. It must be the morning front desk worker.

"Morning," Samantha says.

"Samantha, ask to speak to the owner. His name is Winston Alpine. Pretend you need to talk to him about your membership."

"Okay," she says to me, making me cringe.

"Excuse me?" the woman answers.

"Oh, um, I meant I'd like to talk to Mr. Alspine."

"You mean Mr. Alpine?" the woman asks.

"Yes," I say.

"Yes," Samantha repeats.

"May I ask what this is about?"

"Your membership," I tell Samantha.

"Your membership. I mean, my membership. Mine."

I suppose this could be going worse, but it's off to a pretty bad start.

"I see. Are you not satisfied with your membership?" the woman asks.

"Tell her you have to miss several months because

you're pregnant, and you're hoping you can have your membership paused until after the baby is born."

"Ooh, that's a great idea," Samantha says, making me think she clearly forgot to take her super vitamins this morning.

"Samantha, talk to the woman, not me!"

"Right. I just had this great idea. You see I'm pregnant." There's a pause, and part of me wonders if Samantha is showing this woman her belly. "So I wanted to see if I could put my membership on hold since I won't be able to use it until after the baby is born."

"That shouldn't be an issue, but you will need Mr. Alpine to approve the request before it can be put through. Let me go see if he's available."

There's another pause, and then Samantha says, "She's gone, Jo. How am I doing?"

I can't tell her the truth, so I opt for, "Just fine. But when you get into Mr. Alpine's office, I'll need you to try to work Sabrina into the conversation."

"How do I do that?"

"I'll help you. Don't worry."

"Mr. Alpine is available to see you now," the woman says. "Follow me."

I can hear the woman's shoes clicking on the floor. Why do all the front desk workers wear heels with their workout attire? It's ridiculous.

"I like your shoes," Samantha says. "I'm stuck in flats until the baby is born."

"Ugh, that's a bummer. I always wear heels. They

make your legs look ten times more muscular and defined."

Camille and Sabrina both heard clicking on Thursday night. Could it have been the clicking of this woman's heels?

"Samantha, ask her what her name is," I say.

"What's your name?"

"Melanie. What's yours?"

"Sam."

"I haven't seen you here before, Sam. Do you usually come in the evenings?"

"Yes. Say yes!" I say.

"Yes. I work during the day. I took the morning off, though."

"Don't mention Quentin, Sam. Don't let her know anything else about you." She might be talking to the killer.

"Why?" Samantha asks, and I know she's talking to me, but the woman answers anyway.

"Why did I ask if you come in the evenings? I work mornings. At least most of the time. I do fill in some evenings when Tasha calls out sick, though."

"Ask her if she worked last Thursday evening, the night of the storm," I say.

"Did you work last Thursday?"

"Yeah, I did. Why?"

She was there! She was the front desk girl. Camille told us the front desk girl left early, but what if she didn't?

What if she stayed and waited to kill Sabrina after Camille left?

"Sam, tell her you skipped that night because of the storm."

"I didn't come that night because of the storm."

"Yeah, good thing, too. One of our employees was found dead the next morning," the woman says.

"Ask her when she left."

"When did you leave?"

"I left early. I wanted to get home before the storm got bad."

"Samantha, ask her if she knows Camille," I say.

"Do you know Camille?"

"No. Should I?"

"Tell her she was one of Sabrina's clients," I say.

Samantha repeats what I said.

"Oh. The poor woman is probably getting grilled by the cops then. I know they called me to the station to find out when I left and if I saw anyone outside."

"Did you?" Samantha asks without me prompting her.

"No, but with no power, the doors couldn't lock unless someone manually locked them with a key. I don't know what time Sabrina did that. I left before her and the woman she was training."

While this is helpful, I can't read the woman's expressions or body language to try to determine if she's telling the truth.

"Where are we?" Samantha asks.

"Mr. Alpine's office is in the basement," the woman says.

My heart starts racing. "Sam, get out of there. She might be the killer. Don't go to the basement. Tell her you need to use the restroom and head for the nearest exit."

"I-I have to use the bathroom," Samantha says, sounding really panicked.

"There's one right next to Mr. Alpine's office," the woman says.

"Sam, turn around!" I practically yell.

"I—"

The call ends.

CHAPTER FOURTEEN

"Sam!" I yell.

Cam rushes into the kitchen. "What happened?"

"I don't know. The call just ended." I jump to my feet as I redial Samantha's number. It goes straight to voice mail. "I think she's in trouble. She won't pick up. She might be with the killer, Cam."

"Let's go. I'll drive."

Cam and I rush out with barely a word to Jamar. Right now, I can't worry about leaving him to cover Cup of Jo alone. I have to get to Samantha. I'm the one who put her in danger. Whatever happens to her and her baby is my fault.

Cam reaches for my hand and squeezes it. "Don't think the worst. We should call Quentin."

"If I call him, I'll have to tell him everything."

"I get that you don't want to do that, but if Sam's life is on the line, you don't have a choice."

I nod and pull out my phone. I try Sam again first, but it goes directly to voice mail just like last time. I dial Quentin.

"Detective Perry."

"Quentin, it's me. Sam is in trouble. She's at the gym. We were on the phone, and the line went dead. She was talking to the front desk worker. Melanie is her name. I know you don't want me working on this case, but Sam said you needed me, and I agreed to help her."

I hear his shoes on the floor. He's running. Then I hear the car engine start. "I'm out of the station. We can talk freely now. Tell me everything that happened."

I fill him in. "I'm sorry, Quentin. I never meant for her to get hurt. This was her idea. She was trying to help you."

"You said you were done. Why couldn't you stay out of it? If anything happens to Sam or the baby—"

"I know. I feel awful, Quentin. Please get to the gym and save them."

He hangs up on me.

Cam squeezes my leg, and I realize we're parked in front of the gym. Quentin's patrol car comes whipping into the spot next to ours, the siren blaring. He jumps out and pounds on the gym door, his badge pressed to the window.

Cam and I hurry to catch up to him, but I don't dare say a word. He has a gun, and right now I don't trust him not to use it. I've never seen him look so angry.

A woman opens the door. "What's this about?" she asks, and I recognize her voice.

"That's Melanie," I say.

"Do I know you?" she asks me.

"Where's my wife?" Quentin growls.

"The woman you took to the basement," I clarify. "Where is she?"

"In Mr. Alpine's office. Why? What is going on?"

Quentin pushes his way into the gym, and Cam and I follow. "Bring me there now, and so help me if a single hair is out of place on my wife's head—"

"Detective!" I say in the sternest voice I can muster. If he threatens this woman's life, it will get back to the chief. "I'm sure this woman would be happy to take us to Samantha."

Melanie meets my gaze. "Of course, follow me." She leads us through the hallway, across the gym, and then down a set of stairs. Mr. Alpine's office really is down in the basement.

"I was on the phone with the woman you brought down here," I say, descending the steps. "She sounded distressed, and then the call ended. You can see why her husband is upset."

"There's no cell reception down here. It's a dead zone. I'm sure the call just dropped."

Quentin glares at me. I'd think he'd be happy to hear that. It means Samantha is most likely fine.

Melanie brings us to a door and knocks. "Mr. Alpine, there's a detective here to see you."

"Come in," comes the voice on the other side of the door.

Melanie opens the door and steps into the office. Samantha is seated across from Mr. Alpine, a clipboard in her hand. She turns to look at us, and her eyes widen.

"Quentin, Jo, what are you both doing here? Together?"

Mr. Alpine stands up. "What is she doing here?" He jabs a finger in my direction.

Yeah, I forgot I wouldn't be welcomed with open arms.

Cam wraps a protective arm around me, while Quentin completely ignores Mr. Alpine and bends down in front of Samantha.

"Sam, sweetie, are you okay? Jo told me you sounded like you were in trouble." He brushes a stray piece of hair from her face.

"I was doing fine, but I can't understand a word of this contract amendment." She holds up the clipboard.

"What contract amendment? What is this?" Quentin asks, looking at Mr. Alpine.

"I'm not answering anything until you tell me why you brought that woman back here after she impersonated one of my employees." Mr. Alpine crosses his arms.

Quentin stands up. "This is a murder investigation. I'm not at liberty to share any information with you at this time. Now, Sam and I will be leaving. Sam, you can bring that contract. We'll go over it at home together."

Quentin helps Sam to her feet and then motions for Cam and me to leave the office first.

"Hold on," Mr. Alpine calls after us. When we don't stop, he follows us. "I think I should be updated on this case. After all, the murder occurred on my property."

"You're right about that," I say. "And there's a good chance that one of your employees, or maybe even you, is the murderer."

"What?" Mr. Alpine shrieks, rushing ahead of us to block the stairwell. "I didn't kill anybody, and my staff would never do such a thing either. Everyone liked Sabrina. There were no conflicts between her and anyone else here."

"What about you?" I ask Melanie. "Camille Abrams said she and Sabrina heard clicking when she was leaving the gym during the power outage. Clicking like heels would make on this floor." I motion to her shoes.

Melanie looks petrified.

Quentin turns to her. "What time did you leave the gym?" he asks.

"I don't remember. The power went out, and Sabrina called me at the front desk. She told me to go home."

"The phone system wouldn't have worked if the power was out," Mr. Alpine says.

"No, what I mean is I was at the front desk. She called my cell."

"Sabrina had your cell phone number?" I ask. "Were you two friends outside of work?" I don't see how since Melanie told Samantha she usually works the morning shift, and I know for a fact that Sabrina worked afternoons and evenings.

"Well, no, but she knew there was a storm coming, and she insisted we exchange numbers in case the gym lost power and we needed to talk. Everyone knew the storm was going to be bad. That's why virtually no one was here."

"Did you see anyone else when you left?"

"Just this mother running down the street with her stroller. The poor baby must have been soaked."

What kind of mother brings their baby out in a storm? Didn't she see the weather forecast? It was all anyone was talking about on Thursday.

"Oh, and this guy was hanging around the coffee truck outside."

"I knew it!" I blurt out. Mac was here Thursday night, and now he's gone. "Quentin, Mac came into Cup of Jo today and made this big show of throwing in the towel and leaving Bennett Falls because his coffee truck failed. He said he couldn't compete with me. But he had already told Cam and me that his truck didn't work because of an issue with the engine."

"Then he would have taken it to the mechanic down the road," Quentin says. "We can go there now and confirm it."

"I want to go home," Samantha says. "I'm tired, and my feet hurt."

"Take her home, Quentin. Cam and I can go to the mechanic."

Quentin looks beyond mad. "I'm taking Sam home. I'll follow up with the mechanic after I drop her off." I'm assuming he doesn't want to have any witnesses to him agreeing to allow Cam and me to interrogate the mechanic, so I just nod.

When we exit the gym, Samantha gives me a small smile. "Thanks for coming to check on me, Jo. I'm sorry I scared you."

"It's okay. It's not your fault." I wave goodbye to her and get into Cam's SUV.

"You two are almost acting like you did in the old days," Cam says.

"She's pregnant. I have to be nice to her."

"You're Jo. You're a nice person." He takes my hand, brings it to his mouth, and kisses the back of it. "And that's just one of the many reasons why I love you so much."

"Really?" I ask as he starts the car and backs out of the parking space. "And what are the many other reasons?"

He pretends to check his watch. "I'm afraid we don't have enough time for me to list them all. We're almost at the mechanic's shop."

"Saved by the forklifts, I suppose."

The mechanic's shop is literally a four-car garage. It looks like there used to be a large home attached to this or at least on the property at one time, but now the grassy area sits empty. Well, nearly empty. There are stacks of used tires.

Cam parks, and we walk across the parking lot, which is dirt by the way, to the regular-sized door to the side of the large garage doors. Cam opens it for me, and we step inside. It looks like a glorified mud room. There's a bench with a coat rack above it on one wall. The other side is lined with a row of lockers, and then the far end has a desk with a burly-looking man seated at it.

"Can I help you?" the man asks us.

"I hope so," Cam says. "We were curious if you recently worked on the coffee truck that used to be parked on this road next to Fantasy Fitness."

"I can tell you the truck was never in here. It wouldn't run, and the owner was too cheap to pay us to tow it here. I had to send two guys over to work on it on the sidewalk."

I'm surprised they'd be willing to do that. "Why didn't you turn down the job?" I ask.

"Because of the place right off Main Street. They get most of the business in town since they have the prime location. I can't afford to be turning away business, no matter how much of a pain a customer might be."

"Makes sense. We own Cup of Jo on Main Street, so we know how tough it can be to run a successful business."

The man cocks his head at us. "You own Cup of Jo, you say?"

"That's correct," Cam says.

"Well, then I dare say you ran that coffee truck right

out of town. He said he couldn't get customers because everyone went to the coffee place on Main Street."

That means Mac told the same story to the mechanic. I guess it's a good idea to stick to one story if you want to make it believable.

I can't think of anything else to ask this man since he already confirmed the story about the engine was true. Mac had to have his truck fixed in order to leave town. "Well, thank you for talking to us," I say.

"Hey, I know you're on Main Street, which is as close as you can get to the other car shop in town, but don't forget about us out here. We do good work, and our prices are very competitive."

"I'll remember that when I need my oil changed next month," I say.

The man tugs down the front bill of his baseball cap slightly in thanks.

Cam and I leave, and since I'm not supposed to discuss the case with Quentin, I decide to text Samantha instead. I let her know the mechanic confirmed Mac's story. But that still doesn't explain why Mac was outside his truck Thursday night. He was at the scene of the crime, and if you ask me, he's looking really guilty right now.

"What are you thinking?" Cam asks as we drive back to Cup of Jo.

"That I can't wait to prove Mac did this and haul him and his stupid coffee truck back to Bennett Falls so he can pay for his crime."

"We still do have other suspects, you know. Speaking of, do you have the address for Sabrina's other Thursday night client? Maybe we should go pay him a visit."

"I guess we should." If for no other reason than to check him off the list of suspects. The more people we eliminate, the more it incriminates Mac. "But let's stop at Cup of Jo first and check on Jamar. He's still on his own, and the lunch crowd will be hitting soon."

Cup of Jo is packed. Poor Jamar looks frazzled.

"Over there." He motions with only his eyes. "That's the new chief of police. He was asking questions about you guys."

I don't have to look up to see him heading our way.

CHAPTER FIFTEEN

Oh, boy. It isn't merely Quentin's job on the line here. I was at the gym again without a membership. And now there are witnesses that have seen Quentin and me questioning gym employees together.

I pull Cam and Jamar into the kitchen. "Jamar, did he happen to go next door first?" I ask.

"Yeah, Robin called to warm me he was on his way in here."

"Then he knows Samantha wasn't at work."

"That doesn't mean he knows Quentin was with her or us," Cam says, rubbing my arms.

"But he's here, and he clearly wants to talk to us considering he made a beeline right for us." I discreetly peer through the window to see Chief Harvey standing at the counter, waiting. I duck down to avoid being caught snooping. "What are we going to do?"

"You could sneak out back," Jamar says. "I can tell

him we ran out of supplies, and you two rushed right out to get them when I told you."

That might work, but I'm not sure avoiding the new chief is the way to go.

"No, I'm not going to run from this man. I have to face him and show him I'm not intimidated by him." Even if I actually am.

"Then I'm going with you," Cam says.

"I would, too, but someone has to run this place." Jamar cracks a smile, and I know he's trying to ease the tension in the kitchen.

"Thanks, Jamar. You really are a lifesaver."

Cam leads the way back out to where Chief Harvey is waiting for us. He cocks his head as the three of us approach him. Jamar gives me an encouraging half smile before walking around the counter to clear some tables.

"You must be the new chief of police," I say, not sure if I want him to know I know his name. He might think Quentin told me.

"Chief Harvey. I know all about you, Ms. Coffee."

I take a deep breath and attempt to casually lean against the counter as I say, "Now, how can you say that? We've just met. Most people in this town have known me since the day I was born."

"That's right," Mrs. Marlow says, walking up behind Chief Harvey. "Jo is a good girl, and I don't care for the way you're looking at her right now."

When Chief Harvey turns to face her, I crack a smile. Have I mentioned I love my town?

"And you are?"

"Part of Jo's family, and it would do you well to remember it. This poor girl has been through enough. It's a wonder she's ever stuck her neck out for the BFPD with that no-good detective running the show. You've heard what he did to her, right? Him and that woman next door."

Well, I wasn't expecting Mrs. Marlow to dump my unfortunate dating life on the guy, although I think I'm starting to see her motive for doing so.

"We'd all be a lot more fortunate if Jo here had decided to go into law enforcement. She's smart, and people open up to her because she has a good heart. Unlike a certain detective."

I don't want her to get Quentin fired in the process of building me up to the chief. "Mrs. Marlow, that's very sweet of you to say, but Detective Perry—for all his faults —is good at his job. We just have different approaches to solving crimes."

"You shouldn't have an approach at all," Chief Harvey says, turning back to me. "You are not an officer of the law, Ms. Coffee. You are a citizen."

"Yes, and isn't it a citizen's duty to report wrongdoings and help the police fight them?" Mrs. Marlow asks, placing her hand on Chief Harvey's arm and forcing him to look at her again. "I don't think you realize where you moved to, Chief Hardly."

I'm sure the butchered name is intentional.

"It's Harvey. Chief Harvey," he corrects her.

Mrs. Marlow waves her free hand in the air, the other hand still clutching the chief's arm. "The point is, we're family here. And when someone messes with one of our family, we're going to get involved. If you ask me, using Jo's help to solve cases is the smartest thing Quentin Perry has ever done. He and Jo might not get along, but neither one of them lets that get in the way of justice being served in this town, because that's the kind of town Bennett Falls is." She finally lets go of his arm now that her speech is finished.

Mickey walks over and wraps an arm around Mrs. Marlow. "So you know, Chief, she speaks for all of us."

Chief Harvey looks dumbstruck. Mrs. Marlow is right. He has no idea where he moved to, but he better learn fast.

I turn around, pour a large dark roast coffee, and add a chocolate stick to it. "Welcome to Bennett Falls, Chief," I say, handing him the cup. "On the house."

The fact that it's a to-go cup isn't lost on him. He nods ever so slightly in my direction before turning on his heel and walking out. The crowd in Cup of Jo remains completely still and quiet until the patrol car drives by on its way down Main Street, taking Chief Harvey with it. Then applause and cheers ring throughout the café.

I hug Mrs. Marlow and whisper, "You've always been my favorite customer."

"I know, dear. I know." She pulls away and pats my cheek.

Robin walks in looking really confused. "What did I miss?" she asks, walking up to the counter.

"Just Mrs. Marlow here putting the new police chief in his place," I say. "She was incredible."

"I couldn't agree more, but we still have a case to solve to show Chief Harvey that Mrs. Marlow's words were correct," Cam says.

He's right. Quentin has to track down Mac and his coffee truck, but we can go talk to Sabrina's other Thursday night client, Austin Jones. We grab some crumb cake to take with us because I can't even remember if I've eaten today, and we head back out. There's a closed sign on Bouquets of Love, so I guess Samantha is taking the rest of the day off. I didn't think to ask Robin what Samantha said when she called her to say she could go back to Cup of Jo.

Austin Jones lives near Lake View, which Cam points out makes it look like he could have easily murdered Sabrina and returned home in no time. He might be right, but I'm still putting my money on Mac. I can't believe I really ran him out of town. There has to be another reason he left. It makes sense that he wound up killing Sabrina for some reason I don't know yet and then fled to avoid being caught.

"You're going to keep an open mind about Austin Jones, right?" Cam asks, taking his eyes off the road briefly to look at me.

"Of course. I plan to get to the bottom of this whether it means I'm right about Mac or not."

Cam reaches over and squeezes my hand. "The thing that strikes me as odd is that no one seems to know why anyone would want to harm Sabrina. She was well liked."

"You're right. But yet, she doesn't seem to have had any friends."

"Maybe she was a loner. Growing up in foster care could mean she was hesitant to form lasting relationships. She was bopped around from home to home. She most likely didn't want to form attachments to anyone, even as an adult, for fear of being tossed aside again."

"That's really sad. It would also mean her only long-term relationships were with her clients at the gym."

"Camille and Austin," Cam says. "I think you're right. Camille seemed genuine when we talked to her, so maybe Austin had a thing for Sabrina, and she rejected him."

"That's one theory," I say.

Cam sighs. "You're still going with Mac as the killer."

"I can't help it. Sabrina saw him every day. So there's another relationship. But he owned a coffee truck. It's mobile. He could pick up and leave at any time."

"Which he did."

"So maybe she saw him as a risk. He could have pursued a relationship with her, and she turned him down because she was afraid he'd pick up and leave town."

"He had about fifteen years on Sabrina," Cam points out.

"So? Sabrina grew up without parents or any close relationships. I'm not sure something like age would matter to her, and at the point she was in her life, is fifteen years that big of a deal?"

"Probably not," Cam concedes. "Okay, I admit you make a good case against Mac, but there's still no proof.

Which is why I need to go back to the gym after talking to Austin. I want to check the back exit from the women's locker room. It's not possible that the killer didn't leave anything behind to identify them.

Cam pulls up to the red brick home on Lake View. From the driveway, I can actually see the back of the gym. I get out of the SUV and stare at the gym.

"That looks like the exit from the locker rooms," I say, pointing.

Cam follows my gaze. "You're right. Austin could have exited through the women's locker room and run back home." He has that look, like he thinks this case will be solved as soon as we talk to Austin. I'm not so sure, though.

"It's odd how three things in this case have all lined up on this road. First the gym, then the mechanic, and now Austin's house."

"Yet the mechanic and Austin aren't connected," Cam says.

"No, they're not. And Austin might not be connected to Sabrina's murder either."

He bobs his head. "I promise not to jump to conclusions if you don't."

"You mean if I stop," I say.

He laces his fingers through mine as we walk up to the front door. "You always know what I'm thinking."

"Usually, yes." I laugh.

He rings the doorbell.

I didn't look into Austin to find out what he does for a living. There's a good chance he's at work right now. It would explain why he goes to the gym in the evenings. To my surprise, the front door opens, and the man inside is drying his hair with a towel. Thankfully, he's dressed.

"Can I help you?" His gaze volleys between Cam and me.

"I hope so. I'm Joanna Coffee, and this is Camden Turner. We own Cup of Jo on Main Street."

He furrows his brow. "I'm not sure why two coffee shop owners would come to my house."

"We're actually looking into the murder of Sabrina Kincade. We know you were one of her Thursday night clients."

"Oh, yeah."

"Were you at the gym last Thursday evening?"

"I went earlier than usual because of the storm. I'm an electrician, and the jobsite I was on shut down early for the day. I called Sabrina and asked if she could fit me in early so I could be home before the power went out."

An electrician wouldn't need a storm to take out the gym's power. He easily could have cut the power himself or even gotten past the security system another way. But I promised Cam I would keep an open mind, and I suppose a power outage would be beneficial to someone in Austin's line of work because it wouldn't make people suspect him. It would be a good cover-up. Cam would be so proud if he could hear the thoughts inside my head right now.

"What time did you leave the gym?" Cam asks him.

"I think it was between eight and eight-thirty. After my workout with Sabrina, I swam laps in the pool."

"The gym has a pool?" I ask.

"Yeah, it's past the locker rooms. You can't miss it."

But I did. "Why did you stay so late if you moved your training session to earlier?"

"The storm hadn't started yet. I kept an eye on my weather app. They kept pushing it back, so I decided to swim for a while."

"Did you go right home after swimming?" Cam asks.

Austin doesn't answer right away, and I find his hesitation quite suspicious.

"You stuck around. Why?"

"I know how this is going to look, but it's not what you think."

"What is it then?" I ask.

He takes a deep breath. "I had a thing for Sabrina, but she was always turning me down. I asked her out again Thursday evening. She said no, like always, and told me she had another client to see. I thought she was blowing me off."

"You didn't know she was scheduled to train Camille Abrams?" I ask.

"No. I thought I was her only Thursday night individual client. She teaches classes before she sees me. Self-defense classes."

"So what did you do?" I ask.

"I waited outside until it was about time for the gym to close. I wanted to catch her on her way out."

I was wrong. It wasn't Mac on the sidewalk at all. It was Austin. He was upset with Sabrina, and he waited until she was done with her shift so he could corner her. "You're the one Melanie saw by the coffee truck Thursday night. You stayed to confront Sabrina."

CHAPTER SIXTEEN

"Melanie? Oh, the front desk girl." Austin nods. "Yeah, I admit it. I was there. I was waiting for Sabrina. I figured she'd cut out of work when the power was out. I was going to offer her a ride home because I'm a nice guy."

A *nice* guy who harassed Sabrina every chance he got. The man clearly needs to spend some time with an online dictionary because he doesn't know the meaning of the word nice. He didn't swim laps because the storm was pushed back. He didn't want to leave the gym until he knew Sabrina would. He was biding his time without looking suspicious. Until he went outside.

"Did you go back inside the gym?" I ask. He could have easily walked in, much like anyone else could have after the power went out. At least until Sabrina locked the door behind Camille. But what about the door from the locker room? Was that manually locked as well? Probably not. That has to be how the killer got inside, if he or she wasn't already inside when the power went out. But that doesn't help me figure out who it was. It doesn't tell me much of anything at all.

"I was going to, but I saw that woman come out. The one you mentioned Sabrina was working with. And Sabrina locked the door when she saw me."

That must have made him angry. "Is that when you realized you'd have to find another way in? Maybe through the women's locker room?"

"What? No! I didn't go back inside. I went home."

"Can anyone verify that story?"

"Of course not. I was alone. The storm had really kicked up by then. The only other person I saw besides Camille and Sabrina was the lady with the baby stroller."

Melanie mentioned that woman. Austin saw her, too? What was she still doing out in the rain? Unless she was trying to take shelter waiting for a ride to come pick her up.

"Did you see Sabrina again that night?" I ask.

"No. I swear. I came right home."

He doesn't have an alibi, but without proof, Quentin will never be able to pin this on Austin simply because Austin was rejected by Sabrina.

"Did you walk home?" Cam asks.

"No, I had my car. I went to the gym straight from work."

"Wait a minute," I say. "Something isn't adding up. You said you asked Sabrina to train you earlier than usual because of the storm, but you also said she taught self-defense classes before your training sessions. So wouldn't she be unable to move up your training?"

"Okay, fine. We met at our usual time. I asked her to see me early, and she said she couldn't. But I saw her class. There were like two people there. She could have canceled it for me." His tone is filled with bitterness. "She always said no to everything. Dinner, a movie, even coffee. I mean who can't make time for coffee?"

Someone who wanted nothing to do with him. "It sounds to me like she didn't want to lead you on," I say.

"Yeah, well it sounded to me like she was a prude. She never dated anyone. It was like she thought she was too good for the world."

"You don't know a thing about her childhood, do you?" Cam asks. "Because if you did know how rough Sabrina had it growing up, you'd never say such awful things about her. She had a lot of trust issues, and you were a complete stranger to her. How long had you even been working with her?"

"A few months." Austin scowls. "You know what? I don't have to talk to you people. You're not cops, and I didn't do anything wrong." He slams the door in our faces.

"I don't think he liked where that conversation was going," Cam says. "We should let Quentin know that Austin wasn't only there that night, but that he had a grudge against Sabrina." He takes out his phone to make the call. I'm usually the one who gets in touch with Quentin, but I guess with the chief so insistent that I, specifically, keep my distance from Quentin when he's working a case, Cam feels it's best if he contacts him. But before he can dial, the phone rings.

"It's Jamar," he says as we get back into the SUV. He starts the engine and waits for the call to connect to the Bluetooth before answering. "What's up, Jamar?"

"Cam, we've got a problem. Something's going on with the stove," Jamar says. "It just started smoking. I didn't even know it was on. There's nothing in the oven, though."

"Turn off the power to the oven. I'll be right there," Cam says, backing out of the driveway. He ends the call and turns to me. "I hate to cut this short, but I can't lose my oven."

"Drop me off at the gym. I'll investigate, and you can go handle the issue with the oven. You can pick me up when you've made sure everything is okay in your kitchen."

"Are you sure?" He clearly doesn't like the idea of leaving me alone where a murder took place, but who would do anything to me in broad daylight?

"I'll be fine. There are workers and clients in the gym. It's not like I'll be on my own."

To my surprise, he pulls up to the sidewalk in front of the gym. "I'll have my phone on me. Call me if you need anything." He leans over and kisses me.

"I will. Good luck."

"Right back at ya."

I get out and close the door. Cam hesitates for a

moment before driving off. We can't afford to lose the oven. It would cost a fortune to replace it. Cup of Jo is doing well, but Cam and I aren't exactly rolling in money. Not with the loans we have to repay.

I walk around to the back of the gym, looking for the exits from the locker rooms. To my surprise, there are no keycard readers back here, which means you can exit through the locker rooms, but you can't enter the building through them. This isn't how the killer got inside the gym. There goes that theory.

I search the parking lot, looking for anything the killer might have left behind when he fled. The chances of finding anything days later, and after that brutal storm with the lashing rain, are close to nil. The rain probably washed away any evidence.

I walk back around to the front of the building and pause where the coffee truck used to be. It has to be Mac. There's no other explanation. A woman with a stroller walks by, and as she goes, something falls out of the back of the stroller.

"Ma'am, you dropped something." I hurry over and scoop up the stuffed frog.

She turns and says, "Oh, I didn't even realize. Thank you."

I bring the toy back to her but don't give it to the baby. It was on the ground after all. It should probably be washed or at least disinfected. "It got a little dirty," I say, handing it to her.

She takes it and puts it in the back compartment on

the stroller. "This thing gets washed on a daily basis just about. He's always throwing it out of the stroller. I don't even know why I bother giving it to him. Maybe he doesn't like frogs." She gives a short laugh.

"Maybe," I say. "How old is he?"

"Fifteen months."

I don't know why, but it's always seemed odd to me that people measure babies' ages by months. Why not say he's a year old? I tell people I'm thirty, not however many months that equates to. I do some quick mental math and realize it's over 360 months! Yikes.

"Anyway, we were out for our daily walk and wondering where the coffee truck went."

"Oh, I heard he left town," I say.

"Well, that's a bummer. I was getting coffee there every day. I need it to stay awake since Trevor keeps me up most of the night. He can sleep all day, but I have things to do." She pushes the sun shade on the stroller to better cover the sleeping baby.

"I don't know if it's too far for you, but if your errands ever take you near Main Street, I own Cup of Jo. Stop in. I'll get you a coffee on the house."

"Oh, aren't you sweet? I just might do that." She smiles and then pushes her stroller down the sidewalk. As she walks away, I hear a noise coming from inside her stroller. The baby must have woken up from his nap. Then there's a clicking sound.

I rush after her. "Excuse me."

She slows to a stop. "Yes?"

"Um, that sound," I say. "What is it?"

"What sound?" she asks. "The rattle?" She pulls back slightly on the sun shade, and I see her son is holding a rattle.

"That's not the typical sound a rattle makes," I say.

"No. This one makes two different sounds. The regular rattle when he shakes it and then a clicking if he twists the top. Why?" She squints at me.

Could this be the clicking sound Camille heard? Melanie left before Camille and mentioned seeing a woman with a stroller. What if this woman went inside the gym after that?

"Did you happen to take shelter inside the gym the night of the storm?" I ask.

"Excuse me?" She seems taken aback by my question.

"Last Thursday night. Two people said they saw a woman with a stroller during that storm, and one of the clients said she heard a clicking sound in the gym that night when she left. Was that you? Were you there? Was it your son's rattle the woman heard?"

"Oh." She presses a hand to her chest. "Yes, I did duck inside. We got stuck out in the rain, and I couldn't find anywhere else that was open. My husband told me not to go for my usual walk since there was a storm coming, but he doesn't seem to understand how difficult it can be to lose the baby weight. I walk several times a day. I can't afford not to. Anyway, we stayed inside the gym until my husband came to pick us up."

I guess that makes sense. "Right. Well, it's a good thing the power went out. Those doors are usually locked up tight. You need a keycard to get in."

"Or the override code," she says, stopping me short.

"You know about that?" I ask.

"I used to work there. Before Trevor was born. I was in great shape back then."

Judging by the size of her biceps, she's still in great shape. Carrying a baby around must be a great arm workout.

Oh my goodness! Trevor is fifteen months old! Sabrina started working at the gym two years ago when someone left on maternity leave. Two years ago would have been when Erin found out she was pregnant. This is the woman whose job Sabrina took!

"Do you like being a stay-at-home mom?" I ask, trying to sound casual. "It's probably a lot more rewarding than working at the gym."

"I get no sleep, and I have to cater to his every whim. Personally, I preferred the gym," she says, surprising me.

And then I remember something Mac told me about a woman named Erin. "You're Erin," I say.

"Yeah, how did you know that?"

"Mac told me about you. He's the guy who owned the coffee truck."

She looks surprised. "Mac talked to you about me?"

"Yeah, he mentioned you and Sabrina were his two regulars." He also mentioned she was divorced, yet she referred to the person who picked her up Thursday night as her husband. She's lying to me. But why?

Clouds begin to roll in.

"Looks like another storm," Erin says. "How fitting."

"What do you mean?"

A rumble of thunder echoes across the sky, distracting me long enough for Erin to reach inside the stroller. She pulls out a gun and discreetly aims it at me underneath a baby blanket.

CHAPTER SEVENTEEN

If there was a single soul around, I'd scream or do something to draw attention to us, but the gym still isn't back to its usual attendance after the murder, and the storm that's quickly closing in is keeping people off the street.

"Just relax. I don't know what's going on, but there's no need for a gun."

"I know who you are," she says. "You've been poking your nose into this case. You couldn't leave it alone, could you? I even drove that coffee truck out of town for you."

"What?" I ask.

"Here's what's going to happen. You're going to come with me inside the gym."

The gym? Why would she bring me in there? "I don't understand."

"Keep your mouth shut, and do as I say, or I will shoot you before you can blink."

"Okay." I need to get to my phone in my purse. If I

can call Quentin, he can hopefully get here before this crazed woman shoots me.

"If you do anything that alerts anyone of my gun, it will be the last thing you do. Is that clear?"

"Totally clear," I say.

We walk up to the keycard reader, and Erin flips up the panel on the top, revealing a keypad. She types in a code, and I hear the click of the door unlocking.

The front desk woman is the same one who reported me to the police. "Whoa. She's not allowed in here, Erin."

"It's okay, Layla. She's with me."

The gym staff knows Erin because she used to work here. That means they wouldn't find it suspicious if she came back to visit. She could have planned this murder long in advance and maybe even walked right through the front door Thursday night without anyone thinking it was strange at all.

"I'm not sure Mr. Alpine will be okay with it," Layla says.

While Erin is distracted, I discreetly grab my phone and dial Quentin. I muffle the phone at first so no one hears him answer. Then I prop the phone up and hope he can hear what's going on.

"I doubt Mr. Alpine will want me back inside his gym either," I say loudly.

Erin whirls around and shoots me death daggers with her eyes. I'm still baffled at how she's holding me at gun point with her son in the stroller. "She's here to apologize. Isn't that right?"

"Right. That police detective should probably be here, too." That's really going to confuse and possibly anger Erin, but I don't know how else to get Quentin to come here.

"We'll be quick," Erin tells Layla. "Then she turns to me and says, "After you. We're going to the basement."

"The basement. Oh, goody," I say, also loudly enough for Quentin to hear. Erin must really be questioning why I'm talking like this all of a sudden. Or maybe she thinks I'm trying to tip off the gym staff.

She makes me lead the way to the elevator since she can't exactly bring the stroller down the stairs. Once we're alone in the elevator, she raises a panel on the wall and types in a keycode. If I had to guess I'd say the basement office in this gym is like the penthouse suite in a skyscraper. You need a special key or code to access it. She keeps the gun trained on me the entire time, and I need to warn Quentin that she's armed, so I say, "You can put the gun away. It's not like I can run anywhere."

"Yeah, right. Like I'm going to give you any opportunity to get away. No, with Mac gone, I can't exactly pin your murder on him, so we're going to have to change the plan."

"How?"

"I'm thinking you return to the gym one last time to end your own life."

"Why would anyone believe I'd do that? I don't even belong to this gym," I say.

"Maybe not, but you insisted on butting into this investigation. Maybe that's because you killed Sabrina Kincade and were trying to cover your own tracks before the police found any incriminating evidence."

"What reason would I have for killing a woman I'd never met?"

The elevator doors open at the basement level, and she gestures with the gun. "Go."

"I'm going," I say, stepping out into the hallway. I walk down to the door of Mr. Alpine's office. I'm willing to bet he's long gone for the day. Erin would probably know his schedule.

"Get inside. Alpine's not here."

I open the door. "Fine. I'm going into Mr. Alpine's office."

"Why are you narrating?" She shoves me from behind, leaving the stroller with her son still inside out in the hallway.

"You're going to leave him there?" I ask, and that makes me wonder where Trevor was during the actual murder. "Is that what you did when you killed Sabrina? Did you leave him in one of the shower stalls?" It would make a good hiding spot if he remained quiet.

Erin laughs. "I handed Trevor over to his father long before I killed Sabrina. I just had the rattle with me still, and the stupid thing fell out of my pocket. The floor in the coat room is carpeted so I thought I'd be okay, but the thing twisted and made that clicking sound."

That's what Camille heard. And the gym has a coat room? No one would be using it at this time of year, so it made the perfect hiding place for Erin. Even in the dark, no one would stumble upon her in there.

"Then you didn't go to the locker room right away. You waited until Layla left."

She smirks. "Maybe you aren't so bad at this detective stuff after all."

If she really thought I was bad at it, she wouldn't be holding me at gun point. "There's still one thing I can't figure out," I say. "Why did you want to kill Sabrina? What did she ever do to you? You two didn't even work here at the same time."

"This was my job first. Mine. I left to have a baby. How is it fair that Sabrina swooped in here and took all my clients while I was gone?"

Even if that's true, how can she think murder is fair retribution for doing so? This woman is crazy. "Did you try to get your job back?" I ask, wanting to keep her talking so Quentin can get here and arrest her before she actually uses the gun.

"It was my job. I shouldn't have to beg for it back. Mr. Alpine should have held it for me and told Sabrina to get lost after my maternity leave was up."

"Did you even talk to him about it?"

"Don't look at me like that. You don't know anything about me, and you're not going to because this is it for

you. You're never leaving this room. At least not alive."
She raises the gun level with my head.

"Drop the weapon!" Quentin yells, rushing into the
room.

Erin turns so she can see Quentin, but she still keeps
the gun trained on me. Her face is completely red with
anger, and I wouldn't put it past her to pull the trigger
out of sheer anger that her plan was ruined.

"I'm not telling you again. Drop the weapon on the
ground and put your hands behind your back," Quentin
says.

"Officer, I'm so glad you're here. I'm only defending
myself and my baby. She threatened me. I was holding
her until I could call the police."

"Then you should have no problem lowering your
weapon," I say, showing her the flaw in her new plan.

"Right." She lowers her arm but doesn't drop the
weapon. "Arrest that woman. She told me she was going
to help me get my job back, but it turns out my old boss
had charges against her or something. She tricked me.
She was going to steal my baby. She wanted to get us
alone down here in Mr. Alpine's office."

"And you just happen to carry a gun in your baby
stroller?" I ask her. "Nice try." I pull my phone out of my
purse. "I should probably mention that I called Detective
Perry when you were talking to Layla upstairs. He's been
on the other end of this call the entire time." Somehow,
the call didn't drop when I came to the basement.

"I recorded the conversation, too. We have your full

confession, complete with the explanation for why you felt Sabrina needed to die," Quentin says. "Now drop the gun."

"No!" She goes to raise the gun, this time at Quentin.

Without thinking, I lunge at her from behind, knocking us both to the floor. Quentin grabs the gun from her hand, while I pin her down. I'm sitting on her back at this point, and Quentin is staring at me in disbelief. We both know she would have shot him if I didn't tackle her.

"You…"

"Saved your life. Yeah. I couldn't exactly leave Samantha to raise the baby on her own. She'd be expecting me to help her raise the child."

Quentin laughs, but it's only brief, and it's cut short when Erin squirms underneath me.

"This is assault!" she yells. "I want to press charges."

"You'd know all about assault, Erin. You assaulted Sabrina with a fifteen-pound weight all because you thought she'd replaced you at work. What did you think was going to happen when you left on maternity leave? All your clients would sit at home and wait for you to come back? The world goes on."

"They should have waited for me. I'm ten times the instructor Sabrina was. I mean, she taught self-defense, and she couldn't defend herself against me."

"You snuck up on her like a coward," I say.

"Okay, enough," Quentin says, removing his cuffs

and placing them on Erin's wrists. I stand up as he reads her rights and walks her out of the room.

"What about my son?" Erin asks as we walk by the stroller in the hallway.

"Now you think about him?" I scoff. "What did you think would happen when you committed murder?"

"Jo, grab the stroller. We need to bring him back to the station."

"He has a father. My guess is he's supposed to pick up Trevor soon." I grab Erin's purse from the stroller.

"Hey, that's mine!" she protests. "You can't go through my stuff."

"Then tell us Trevor's father's number, and we'll call him." I pull out my phone.

"I'm not handing Trevor over to him," Erin says.

"Quentin, you can bring her to the car. I'll be right behind you with the baby."

He doesn't protest. He turns a blind eye to me going through Erin's belongings. I guess saving his life earned me certain liberties. I wonder how long that will last.

I find Erin's phone, but it's locked, so that won't help me. I take the elevator up to the lobby, looking for anything in Erin's purse that might lead me to finding out who Trevor's father is. When the elevator opens, Layla rushes over to me.

"That detective said Erin killed Sabrina. You were helping him solve the case. That's why you had Sabrina's ID badge, isn't it?"

I nod. "Now if only I had Trevor's dad's number."

"I have it. He was listed as Erin's emergency contact in her employee file. Hold on."

"Thank you." I follow her to the desk. She gets the number and places the call, handing me the phone.

I tell him what happened and that he can meet me at the gym to get his son. Then I spend the next twenty minutes waiting for him to arrive. He seems like a completely normal guy.

He hugs Trevor to him. "I never should have left him with her. I left Erin because I noticed a drastic change in her after Trevor was born. She just snapped. She was a completely different person. I wanted to take Trevor with me, but I had to work during the day. Erin said she'd watch him after I left for work and hand him back off to me once I was done for the day. I never thought she'd do something like this, or I swear I wouldn't have left him in her hands." He's sobbing now.

"You need to go down to the police station and tell that to Detective Perry. He's bringing Erin there now to book her for murder."

The man bobs his head and extends his hand to me. "Thank you. Thank you for protecting my son."

"You're welcome."

I'm walking out when Cam's SUV comes flying into a parking spot. He jumps out of the car and rushes over to me, enveloping me in a hug.

"I'm okay. I promise."

"Quentin called me on his way to the station. He told

me what you did." Cam pushes me away at arm's length. "What were you thinking rushing a woman with a gun?"

"I clearly had a moment of temporary insanity because my only thought was that she was going to kill Quentin, and I was the only one who could stop her."

"You mean you were the only one who could stop someone from dying," he says, and that's when I realize he's right. She would have shot at Quentin, but he also might have shot at her. One or both of them could have died.

"I want to go home," I say.

"Unfortunately, the chief wants to hear your side of the story," Cam tells me.

"Ugh. And here I thought having a gun aimed at my head would be the worst part of my day."

Chief Harvey has me explain everything that happened in detail even though he's already listened to the recording Quentin made of my phone call.

This was one of those cases where I'm not sure if I solved it or if the killer solved it for me. Erin slipped up when she mentioned the key code, and her anger with Sabrina wound up getting the best of her. She told me everything I needed to know. I was lucky to have it all recorded thanks to the call I made to Quentin.

Chief Harvey seems to come to the same conclusion I have. "You have a way of sticking your nose into this police department's business. I'll admit your track record shows you usually wind up getting results, but I have to say it seems like luck helps you out more than good old-fashioned detective work."

"I'd never say I'm not lucky, but I do think I do my share of investigating as well." I'm pushing my luck right now.

"I don't use consultants, Ms. Coffee." He leans his elbows on his desk and steeples his fingers in front of his face. "However, if you happen to come across information that might be pertinent to a case one of my detectives is working on, it's your duty as a citizen of this town to pass that information along to Detective Perry."

Did he just give me permission to keep helping Quentin without coming out and calling it that? I'm not going to question it, so I say, "Of course. Anything to help the fine officers at the BFPD."

"Good. I'm glad we have an understanding. You're free to go."

I jump up and meet Cam at Quentin's desk. "I'm ready to get out of here while the chief sort of has luke warm feelings for me at the moment."

Cam laughs. "You and me both."

"Jo," Quentin says, "thank you. I can't—"

I hold up a hand to stop him. "I know you would have shot her to protect me. I didn't have a gun, so I had to tackle her to protect you. Whether we like it or not, we wind up partnering up on some cases. That's what partners do, right? They have each other's backs."

He nods and swallows so hard I see his throat constrict.

Cam wraps an arm around my shoulders and walks me to his car. "Be honest. You were bummed when you realized Erin was the killer because you wanted it to be Mac, the coffee truck guy, weren't you?"

"Maybe a little bit." I feel my cheeks warm. "I don't know why it bothers me so much that he opened a coffee truck."

"Because you're Jo Coffee. Coffee is your thing."

"It is," I say with a smile.

EPILOGUE

Cup of Jo is even more packed than usual on Wednesday because everyone wants to hear about how I saved Detective Perry's life. Quentin even shows up to tell Mickey and his groupies all about my tackling abilities. They eat it up, and I think Quentin is back in their good graces.

Samantha hugs me so tightly I'm afraid she's going to pop that baby right out of her onto the floor of my coffee shop. I may have been born on the floor of my parents' coffee shop, but I don't plan to follow in their footsteps by having any live births in mine. The day is long, and Mo has to shoo people out at closing time.

"I'm beat," I tell her.

"I know what will perk you up," she says, looking through the window to the kitchen. "You've put your own happiness off long enough, Jo. Tell him how you feel. Woman up, already."

I laugh. "Good night, Mo. Enjoy your date, and tell Wes I said hi."

She hugs me again before leaving.

I lock the door behind her and take a deep breath. Mo's right. I don't need to wait for Cam to propose to me. I can do this. I set up the corner table with a black table cloth and place tea light candles in the center. I brew two Americanos because I need the caffeine to steel my nerves. Once it's all set up, I walk into the kitchen.

"Cam, could you come out here for a moment?" I ask him. To my surprise, he's baking. I thought he'd be cleaning up for the night at this point.

"Sure," he says. "Give me one minute." He pulls a cake out of the oven.

"Okay." I nod and swallow hard. My nerves are actually making me shake. I walk back to the table I set up and sit down, wringing my hands together in my lap.

"Deep breaths, Jo," I mumble under my breath. "You can do this. It's Cam. Why would you be afraid to talk to him?" I mentally roll my eyes at myself. I could ruin my longest friendship and my best relationship with one question. Do I really want to do this? Why is this so difficult?

"Sorry about that," Cam says, walking out of the kitchen. He pauses when he sees the table set. "What's going on?"

I take a sip of my Americano to get my brain working enough to form words. "I thought we could take a moment to celebrate."

"You mean solving the case?" he asks, taking a seat across from me.

"That and our success here." I motion to the coffee shop.

"You sound almost surprised this worked out so well." He reaches for my hand. "Why is it you're always surprised at what a great team we make?"

I lower my gaze to the coffee in front of me. "You've known from the start."

He bobs one shoulder. "I'm exceptionally bright," he teases.

"You are. You're a great business owner, the best friend I could ever ask for, and the greatest boyfriend, too. I don't know what I'd ever do without you." It's like once I start talking, the words spill out of me. My heart is taking over where my brain was failing. "Cam, I can't imagine—"

"Hold on," he says. "I'll be right back."

I stare at him in confusion as he gets up and walks away in the middle of my heartfelt speech. My heart starts racing. I found the nerve to do this once, but I don't know if I can start over.

Cam returns with a glass of water and a piece of strawberry shortcake, complete with loads of fresh strawberries and whipped cream. He stopped me to get dessert? You've got to be kidding me. He smiles as he places the plate between us and hands me a fork. "Here. Try this. It's a new recipe with a secret ingredient."

"Cam, I'm really not hungry right now. I wanted to talk to you about something."

"We'll talk, but please try this first." He turns the plate slightly and moves it toward me. "Please, Jo."

I'm not sure why a new recipe is so important. He usually tests his new baked goods out on our regulars, like Mickey and Mrs. Marlow. They love it because they get free food, and they can also take credit for new items appearing on the menu.

"Can this wait a few minutes?" I ask, putting the fork down.

He looks upset for some strange reason. "Just take a bite. A big one. Then you can tell me whatever it is you need to."

This isn't how I pictured this going at all. I was in the moment a few minutes ago. My emotions were pouring out of me, and I felt ready to actually do this, but now...? I'm not sure I even want to go through with it at this point. He's never insisted I do anything like he is now. Is this a side of him he's kept hidden from me all our lives? Is this a sign I'm rushing into things?

"Jo?" he asks, motioning to the cake.

I grab my fork and angrily stab at the center of the cake. "Fine. I'll eat the stupid..." I stop when my fork hits something. "What the...?" I pull the forked bite away from the plate, and my heart nearly stops beating. Sticking out of the cake is a ring. A diamond ring.

"I see you found the secret ingredient," Cam says. He

spins the plate around and removes the ring, which he washes off in the glass of water he brought to the table.

"You planned this? But I was going to... Did you know I was going to propose?" I ask, dumbfounded.

He smiles softly. "Don't be mad, but Mo told me."

I open my mouth to let out a slew of curses at my meddling sister, but Cam holds up a hand to stop me. "Only because I told her I was planning to ask you. She wanted to make sure I beat you to it since she knew you didn't want to be the one to ask. She was trying to help."

Mo's always trying to help in her own "Mo" way. But this moment isn't about her.

Cam takes my hand in his. "Joanna Coffee, I've loved you from the first moment I met you. You've always been the perfect woman for me, and my life wouldn't be complete without you in it. It would be the greatest honor in the world to call you my wife. Will you marry me?"

My eyes are glistening with tears as I choke out, "Yes. Of course, I will."

Cam slides the ring onto my finger before he stands up and pulls me to him. He kisses me and holds me tightly for several seconds.

My head is spinning, and I feel like I've gone through every emotion in the past few minutes. "I can't believe this."

"It will make for a good story."

"What do you mean?"

"Well, I thought you were going to fight me with your

fork when I was trying to propose. You should have seen the way you stabbed that cake." He laughs.

"That's because I was trying to propose to you."

"You haven't even looked at the ring yet," he says.

Because what the ring looks like isn't important. It's the sentiment behind it that means the world to me. I place my hand flat against his chest and stare at the single round chocolate diamond surrounded by tiny diamonds set on a strawberry gold band. I smile. "It reminds me of coffee," I say, tears clouding my vision.

"It reminded me of coffee, too. I didn't even know chocolate diamonds were a thing, but when I saw this ring, it screamed Jo to me."

It's exactly what I would have picked out myself. "Cam, it's absolutely perfect. I didn't even think I'd care what my ring looked like, but this…" I've never been big on jewelry, but I'll make an exception for this ring. "And it fits perfectly."

"Mo told me your ring size."

"Wait, this means she knew you were planning to propose when I was stressing out to her about wanting you to ask me to marry you. How could she keep this from me? I'm her sister."

"Because she loves you and knew how happy you'd be with this surprise." He tilts my face up to kiss me again.

"I am happy. I couldn't be happier, but not because of the ring. Because of you, Cam."

"And I'll see to it that you are this happy every day for the rest of our lives, but I have one request."

"What's that?" I ask.

"You keep your last name. I can't imagine you not being Jo Coffee."

I laugh. I've always found my name kind of absurd since I'm essentially named Coffee Coffee, but he's right. "I agree. I'll always be Jo Coffee."

"I wouldn't have it any other way," he says before kissing me again.

If you enjoyed the book, please consider leaving a review. And look for *Doppios and Death*, coming soon!

You can stay up-to-date on all of Kelly's releases by subscribing to her newsletter: http://bit.ly/2pvYT07

A Vision in Time Saves Nine

Never Smite the Psychic That Reads You

There's No Crime Like the Prescient

Fight Fire with Foresight

Something Old, Something New, Something Foretold, Corpse So Blue

Madison Kramer Mystery Series

Manuscripts and Murder

Sequels and Serial Killers

Fiction and Felonies

Paranormal YA Books

Touch of Death (Touch of Death #1)

Stalked by Death (Touch of Death #2)

Face of Death (Touch of Death #3)

The Monster Within (The Monster Within #1)

The Darkness Within (The Monster Within #2)

Into the Fire (Into the Fire #1)

Out of the Ashes (Into the Fire #2)

Up in Flames (Into the Fire #3)

Unseen Evil

Evil Unleashed

Fading Into the Shadows

Dark Destiny

The Day I Died

Replica

Writing as *USA Today* Bestselling Author Ashelyn Drake

The One for Me

The Time for Us

Second Chance Summer

It Was Always You (Love Chronicles #1)

I Belong With You (Love Chronicles #2)

Since I Found You (Love Chronicles #3)

Reignited

After Loving You (New Adult romance)

Campus Crush (New Adult romance)

Falling For You (Free prequel to *Perfect For You*)

Perfect For You (Young Adult contemporary romance)

Our Little Secret (Young Adult contemporary romance)

ACKNOWLEDGMENTS

More thanks to my incredible team who makes publishing possible. Patricia Bradley, working with you is always amazing. Thank you for all your insights. Ali Winters at Red Umbrella Graphic Designs, I couldn't have more fun working with you on these covers. Thank you for all you do. To my VIP reader group, Kelly's Cozy Corner, and my ARC team, thank you for supporting me and my books.

To my family and friends, thank you for continuing to ask about my books and offer your support. And to my readers (YOU!), thank you for choosing my books out of all the amazing stories there are to read.

ABOUT THE AUTHOR

Kelly Hashway fully admits to being one of the most accident-prone people on the planet, but luckily, she gets to write about female sleuths who are much more coordinated than she is. Maybe it was growing up watching *Murder, She Wrote* that instilled a love of mystery, but she spends her days writing cozy mysteries. Kelly's also a sucker for first love, which is why she writes romance under the pen name Ashelyn Drake. When she's not writing, Kelly works as an editor and also as Mom, which she believes is a job title that deserves to be capitalized.

 facebook.com/KellyHashwayCozyMysteryAuthor

 twitter.com/kellyhashway

 instagram.com/khashway

 bookbub.com/authors/kelly-hashway

CPSIA information can be obtained
at www.ICGtesting.com
Printed in the USA
BVHW042245151122
651982BV00018B/847/J